Sweet Suspicion

The Pupcake Mystery Series
Book One

By Mary B. Barbee

Mystic Valley Press

Cover Design by Daniela Colleo of Stunning Book Covers

https://marybbarbee.com

To Valentino, my own little sleuthing sidekick.

Chapter 1

E liza grabbed the small pink towel thrown carelessly on the handle of the treadmill in front of her. She dabbed the sweat from her forehead, passed the worn terry cloth along the back of her neck under her loose ponytail, and tucked it back in place on the machine.

Pushing the speed up button a few times, she tried to ignore her heaving chest and sore leg muscles. Taking a few months off of her workout routine impacted her more than she'd like to admit. She was determined to beat her time from yesterday but more importantly, she hoped the increased speed would serve as a distraction from thinking about the strange email she read just before her daily run.

Eliza intentionally shifted her thoughts to the long list of things she would have to do at the shop to start the day. Keeping her pace, she opened her phone to her favorite task list app. She propped the phone in front of her in the slot where a book would have been during her runs years ago.

Reading the last item on the list, Eliza's mind immediately switched back to the creepy email. She shook her head and rolled her eyes, recognizing that she was again struggling to simply let things go. Besides, her life was way too busy to get caught up in another amateur detective case like the one from just a few weeks earlier when someone attempted to sabotage her entry in the Stillson County Fair's baking competition. Although she enjoyed a good classic whodunit book or movie, Eliza truly preferred a simple uneventful life.

The dashboard of the treadmill climbed to three miles, and Eliza exhaled a sigh of relief as she pushed the stop button and stepped off to stretch her calves. Eliza's sweet chihuahua, Pupcake, entered the room and let out a sigh as if he were mimicking his favorite person. He sat and patiently watched as Eliza stretched her calves and gulped down the last few drops of her workout drink.

"Well, hello there, Mister," Eliza grinned. "I guess you heard the machine cut off," she giggled. "I know what you're waiting for." She reached down to give him a little scratch behind his ears. No doubt that Pupcake knew when Eliza finished her workout, she would make a protein shake, and he would get a small taste of the almond butter that she added in very last.

"Let's go, Silly Boy," she said, as she walked past him and led the way to the kitchen.

Pupcake followed right on Eliza's heels, his tail wagging from side to side with excitement.

Eliza's husband, Dean, was sitting at the kitchen table, reading the newspaper and munching on a cinnamon raisin bagel.

"Good morning," he said cheerfully, setting the paper down and taking a sip from his black coffee. "How was the run?"

"Ugh...it's still so hard," Eliza groaned. "Every day, I just can't believe how badly out of shape I have become. That's what I get for pushing it ALL the way down on the priority list for the past few months." She leaned over Dean's shoulder and planted a kiss on his cheek. "But, yes, good morning, my love. How'd you sleep?"

"You're doing amazing, as always, dear, managing all the things you have going on. Don't be so hard on yourself. You'll beat your PR in no time." Dean winked at his wife and stood to put his empty plate in the sink. "I slept like a baby. How about you?"

"Not bad, actually. I have a lot on my mind already today, though. I got this weird email this morning..."

Dean leaned against the counter, emptying his coffee mug with one last long gulp. His eyebrows raised in curiosity.

Opening the refrigerator to retrieve the carton of almond milk from the refrigerator door, Eliza continued, "Yeah, at first I thought it was just a marketing thing. The message didn't land in spam though, so I opened it. The subject line was something like, *Your bad Yelp review*." Eliza bent over and pulled the freezer open and grabbed a frozen banana from the corner where she kept all the fruit.

"Did you get a bad Yelp review?" Dean asked. He began rinsing his empty mug in the kitchen sink.

Eliza nodded. "Yeah, I guess so," she said after Dean set his mug in the dishwasher and turned off the water.

"What did it say?"

"The review or the email?" Eliza asked, now distracted with deciding between chocolate or vanilla protein powder.

"Both," Dean chuckled. "You're the worst story teller, dear," he teased her.

"Oh, sorry," Eliza said, selecting the chocolate flavor and setting it on the counter next to the blender. She turned around and faced her husband, in an attempt to be more present.

"But yes, I did get a bad review. It was my first bad review so far, and it said that my coffee tasted like poison."

She shrugged her shoulders and tried to blow it off, but there was no denying that discovering the comment earlier that morning felt like a gut punch.

"What?!" Dean exclaimed, "That's crazy!" His blue eyes narrowed.

"I know," Eliza said, swallowing hard before continuing with a tone that she hoped would convince Dean that it didn't bother her. "But, honestly, businesses get bad reviews all the time. I read somewhere that the first one is hard, but also, that it's to be expected.

Not everyone likes a peach, I remember that's the phrase I read."

Dean approached his wife and wrapped his arms around her in a warm embrace. "Well, I love peaches," his cheek against hers. "And everyone knows your coffee is delicious. I'm sorry they said that rubbish." He snuck a quick peck on the cheek.

Eliza leaned into the warm hug. She allowed herself to melt in her husband's strong arms and rested her head on his shoulder. She was sweaty and hot, but she didn't care. A hug from Dean was exactly what she needed. Her concerns instantly felt lighter.

"Thanks, love," she said, raising her head from his shoulder and gently pulling away. "But, I need to make my protein shake and jump in the shower, or I'm going to be late. You know how worried Susan gets if I'm running even a minute behind schedule."

Susan Morris was Eliza's best friend who had recently started working at The Pupcake Café, helping Eliza with the morning rush. They had first met when their children were very young playmates, and Eliza was confident their friendship was one that would last a lifetime. However, things had also felt rather challenging lately. Susan was overly protective of Eliza and constantly worried about her working too much or not eating well. It was endearing to a certain point, but every once in a while, it would feel obsessive and would just drive Eliza crazy.

A friendly conversation about that was probably overdue, but Eliza was avoiding it. Besides the fact that she knew Susan had only good intentions, Eliza was also careful not to add much stress to her friend's life. Recently, Susan and her husband, Jason, had decided to separate and had started the divorce process. Although it sounded and appeared like their relationship was remaining amicable, Eliza knew it had to be taking a heavy toll on her friend. She, herself, couldn't imagine a life without Dean, especially after twenty-five years of marriage and children that only recently started lives of their own.

Eliza dropped a scoop of almond butter into the blender on top of everything else and closed the lid. Just as she was about to push the smoothie button, Pupcake let out a short tiny whimper.

"Oh, I'm so sorry, Sir," Eliza said. "How could I forget your share?" She used her finger to clean off the spoon and bent down to hold it out for him. His tongue moved fast, cleaning her finger in record time, as if he hadn't eaten in days.

"Now, if you don't mind, I'll make my smoothie," she laughed as she rose and started the blender.

Dean poured the remaining liquid from the coffee pot into his favorite Yeti travel mug, and Eliza watched from across the kitchen as he meticulously washed and dried the coffee pot. Even now, Eliza counted herself the luckiest girl alive to be married to Mr. Dean Campbell. She was still so in love with her husband. He was her confidante, her biggest cheerleader, and he wasn't hard on the eyes either. As a matter of fact, Eliza thought Dean looked better and better every year. He had a great head of hair for a man in his fifties, and she loved how his salt and pepper hair accentuated his sky blue eyes. She would never stop enjoying just watching him as he sat and read a book, played on the floor with Pupcake, tinkered with projects around the house, or spent time in the garden. She loved it all.

As if he felt her eyes on him, Dean turned and met Eliza's gaze with a big smile. "I think your smoothie is probably done," he said loudly, to be heard over the blender.

"Oh!" Eliza exclaimed and turned back to the blender, shutting it off and unplugging it from the wall. She pulled one of the large green plastic cups from the top of the cupboard and poured her smoothie, filling the cup all the way to the top.

"You didn't tell me what the email said," Dean reminded Eliza as he pushed the dishwasher door shut.

Eliza bent down and scooped Pupcake up into her arms. He began licking her face, no doubt enjoying the salty taste of her sweat.

"Okay, okay," Eliza said to Pupcake, "no more kisses, please." She opened the back door and set him down on the back porch. Watching as he trotted off to find the perfect spot to go potty, she felt a sort of uneasiness return to her stomach. She turned back to Dean.

"So, the review said the shop's coffee tasted like poison," she took a quick breath before continuing. "And like I told you, the subject line of the email was, *Your bad Yelp review*." Eliza locked her eyes with Dean's.

"When I opened the email, it said something like, *Fair warning...* and then something like, *watch your back*."

Dean's eyebrows raised again - this time in shock.

"What, it said something like that, or exactly that?" Dean asked pointedly.

Eliza paused and took a deep breath before she answered. She had hoped it would just go away or that Dean would say she was overthinking things, but his obvious concern was proof that she wasn't overreacting.

"It said exactly that: *Fair warning. Watch your back*," she answered. The pit in her stomach grew as she watched Dean's striking blue eyes fill with worry.

Chapter 2

Eliza parked her little red Toyota Prius in the same spot in the small lot behind The Pupcake Café every day. This morning, she drove there on autopilot, still distracted with the threatening email she had received. Dean had insisted she forward the message to him before she left the house, and he volunteered to stop by the police station to discuss it with Copeland's Chief of Police, Joe Mason, on his lunch break. Dean and Joe had attended the same primary school, but they weren't buddies when they were younger. Now, Dean was a personal injury attorney and the mens' worlds would often collide, resulting in the blossoming of a close and trusting friendship.

Eliza sat in her parked car, shuffling through her purse to find the keys to the backdoor of the café. Just as she felt the metal keyring at the very bottom of her bag, a loud knock on the window by her ear startled her. Her purse fell to the floorboard on its side, its contents spread out around

Eliza's dingy white Vans tennis shoes. A shriek escaped her lips, followed by an exasperated sigh when she turned to find her friend holding her sides and bent over laughing.

Eliza swung open her car door, her brow crinkled, making the parallel lines just above the bridge of her nose deepen.

"Susan! That is not funny! You know I hate being scared!" Eliza scolded her friend, her hands planted on her hips. Pupcake barked from the car.

Eliza hated practical jokes, and her best friend knew that. She became suddenly aware of a warm heat spreading across her face and neck, and she dropped her hands down to her sides. She wasn't the type to fly off the handle at anyone, especially not a friend, so she made a conscious effort to relax her face and posture and take a breath. Pupcake picked up on this shift, as well, and settled back into his car seat, sitting still, quiet and watching.

"I'm sorry, Ellie, but you shoulda seen your face," Susan said, trying to stifle a giggle. "I just couldn't help myself."

Eliza bit her tongue and chose not to respond, keeping in mind that if she didn't have something nice to say, then it's best to just stay quiet. Instead, she gathered Pupcake into her arms from the car and took the opportunity to nuzzle the back of his neck. Pupcake sneaked in a quick little kiss, and Eliza instantly felt a little better. Between Pupcake and Dean, she was indeed a lucky woman.

"Hi, Puppy-cake!" Susan said, reaching down and rubbing his cheek. "You are the cutest little guy ever!"

Eliza slipped her purse over her shoulder, balancing Pupcake in her arms and gripping her keys in her free hand.

"How's your day going so far, Ellie?" Susan asked, leaning in close to Pupcake's face to get some puppy kisses of her own.

"Ugh," Eliza said. "You're not going to believe what I found this morning." She walked to the back of her car and opened the hatchback to retrieve the grocery bag of ingredients she had brought with her.

"Here, let me hold him," Susan said, ignoring Eliza's comment.

Eliza passed Pupcake to Susan and rifled through the bag of ingredients.

"I feel like I'm forgetting something," she said, glancing at Susan who stood there quietly holding Pupcake."Oh well, I'll look through it again when we get inside."

The three of them headed towards the back door of the shop. Eliza slipped her key in the lock, turned it, and pulled the heavy door open, holding it open for her friend.

"Thank you," Susan said politely, reaching over to switch on the multiple light switches on the wall inside the door.

The Pupcake Café was Eliza's favorite place to be when not at home. She had dreamed of opening a cozy coffee shop, and when her kids grew and left the nest, it was Dean who encouraged her to finally make her dream a reality. The town of Copeland welcomed her new café with open arms, and Eliza enjoyed every bit of work that went into it.

Susan set Pupcake down on the floor and he scurried off to make sure no one had moved his bed from his special spot in the corner of the dining area. Eliza watched as he disappeared around the front counter.

"Mmmm... it still smells like those oatmeal cookies you made yesterday afternoon," Susan said, inhaling deeply with her eyes closed as she slipped a clean apron over her head and tied the strings behind her. "So yummy," she mumbled, pulling her shoulder-length light blonde hair back into a messy bun at the nape of her neck.

Eliza opened one of the small red metal lockers she had acquired from a yard sale and slipped her purse inside. She closed the metal flimsy door and turned to grab a clean apron of her own from the hooks on the opposite wall.

"I wonder if we're going to actually reach seventy degrees today," she said. "If we do, we should be prepared for everyone to be out and about this afternoon. You know how busy things get when the weather starts to get nicer."

Susan grabbed the handles of the grocery bag Eliza had carried into the shop and lifted it onto the chair under where the aprons hung.

"Oh yes," Susan agreed. "We should definitely be prepared for a rush. What do you have in mind for today's goodies?"

Eliza's phone chimed with a text notification. She reached to grab it out of her back pocket.

"Wait, wait... let me guess," Susan said, ignoring that Eliza was now distracted. Susan began to look through the contents of the bag. "We've got ham and gruyère cheese, and some green onions. Well, it doesn't take a detective to know that you're making your delicious quiche."

"Yep," Eliza nodded, her eyes focused on the phone in her hand. "Hang on a second, Laura is texting me."

Good morning, Mom! Just finished my last bio lab! I can't tell you how glad I am that class is over, but I think I might have squeezed out a B in the class. We'll see! Hope your morning is going well - Love you!

Eliza quickly texted back, *Love you too, honey! Great job!*

She slipped her phone back into her pocket before heading towards the large kitchen island that was used for the prep station. Susan had set the bag on the table and was washing her hands.

"I have some broccoli in the cooler. Would you mind grabbing that and start prepping it? I'll work on the pie crust first."

"I'm on it!" Susan said enthusiastically and disappeared in the walk-in cooler at the back of the shop.

"Where's the baby?" Eliza called out. That had become Pupcake's calling card, and sure enough, when she called, he came running from around the front of the bakery case and sat at Eliza's feet.

"Oh, there you are!" Eliza grinned. She loved playing that game with the sweet little guy and couldn't resist the cute look he gave her when he sat at attention. She scooped him up with one hand and carried him to the sink where she grabbed a clean bowl and filled it with water. The two of them made their way to his special spot across the dining area, and Eliza set the bowl down flush against the wall where it would least likely get kicked or knocked over by a café patron.

Pupcake kicked his feet like a little bull to nest the soft gray blanket that was thrown carelessly on top of his flat rectangular bed, creating a perfect little circle. He spun around a few times to make sure it was just right before settling in and resting his chin on the side of his new little nest. His eyes looked up at Eliza before squinting and slowly closing for his first nap of the day. *Well, that didn't take long*, Eliza thought to herself, jealous of Pupcake's ability to get comfortable and fall asleep so quickly.

Eliza glanced around the dining room to make sure she hadn't missed any details when closing up shop the day prior. Everything looked in order. The bookshelves near Pupcake's bed were arranged with magazines on the top shelf, board games on the middle two shelves, and well-worn children's books stacked together at the bottom. A string of fairy lights stretched over the large picture window. She reached behind the bookshelf to switch them on and watched as they came alive, blinking gently.

The tables and chairs were all clean and also in order. She would place simple little vases with one fresh flower in each from the walk-in cooler on each table before she flipped the open sign and unlocked the front door.

The front counter was also tidy, and the black and white tile floor still looked shiny and new. Eliza was always surprised how messy things could get in a day. She always took her time cleaning after closing so that she could focus on food prep in the mornings.

Eliza could hear the familiar melodic sound of Susan humming in the kitchen. The broadway hit, "Oh, What a Beautiful Mornin'" was her song of choice that morning, and Eliza didn't mind it all. She appreciated music and felt it calming and even uplifting. She headed back to join Susan at the prep stations and switched her focus back to the pie crust she was making for the quiche.

Eliza gathered the flour, salt, and shortening and placed them at her prep station. She headed into the cooler to grab the butter next.

"I already got the butter out for you," Susan called out as Eliza's hand just touched the door handle.

"Oh!" Eliza said with surprise. "Thank you."

"Yeah, it's right over here. I already cut it into cubes for you, too," Susan grinned, using her elbow to point to her right where the butter was measured and cubed, just as she said.

"Nice! You're the best, Susan," Eliza said. And she meant it. The scare this morning had annoyed her, but Eliza was ready to turn the day around.

Susan smiled and continued to chop the broccoli into small pieces, just as she knew Eliza preferred them for the quiche.

"Hey, you were saying you found something weird this morning?" Susan phrased the sentence as a question.

"Yeah," Eliza responded, measuring out half a cup of water for her pie crusts. "It was an email."

Susan stopped chopping and turned to look at Eliza, her curiosity piqued. "Well, what did it say?" she asked.

"So, I guess we got a bad Yelp review," Eliza started to explain.

"Oh no!" Susan gasped.

"I mean, it's not a big deal really," Eliza shrugged as she whisked the flour and salt together in a big silver bowl. "I mean, businesses get bad reviews all the time. We can't please everyone."

"How bad was it?" Susan asked, her mouth stretched into a grimace as if she was bracing herself for bad news.

"Well, whoever wrote it said that our coffee tasted like poison."

Susan paused and said, "Well, that's ridiculous. Anyone who knows anything, knows that poison doesn't taste like anything. But, actually, in one of those mystery shows I watch, they said cyanide tastes like bitter almonds... which now that I think about it, coffee would be the best way to disguise that."

Eliza and Susan chuckled, and Eliza made a mental note to remember to share that one with Dean. He would get a kick out of it.

"Right, but I think it's not meant to be taken literally."

"Well, clearly, that was just some ignorant person then," Susan said and turned back to continue chopping. She began scooping up mounds of broccoli and dropping them into a glass measuring cup. "How much broccoli do you need?" she asked.

"Let's do about 6 cups," Eliza responded. "And if you'll grate the cheese next, that would be great." She moved onto adding the butter and shortening to the flour and salt mixture with her pastry cutter.

"Sure!" Susan responded. Eliza loved Susan's attitude. She was always so helpful. She didn't know how she ever ran the shop without her best friend by her side.

"So, okay, we got a bad review," Susan said, her back turned to Eliza as she continued to chop and measure. "Then, was that the email?"

Eliza exhaled slowly before continuing. She hated talking about it, but she was the one who brought it up, and it certainly wasn't a secret.

"Well, no. The email's subject line was something like, *Your bad Yelp review.* And then, when I opened the email, it was actually threatening. It read, *fair warning, watch your back.*"

Susan turned on her heels and faced Eliza, her mouth hung open in shock.

"You're kidding me," she said matter-of-factly.

Eliza shook her head. "I wish I was," she responded, "but I don't think that would be very funny."

"Right?" Susan shook her head. "Who was the email from?"

Eliza shrugged even though Susan had turned away again.

"It wasn't an email address I recognized, Juniper1972 at gmail dot com, I think. Dean is going to take it to the police station at lunch today." Eliza paused as she added ice to the measured water. "But, it's probably not a big deal."

Susan nodded. "Totally," she said. "Let's not put too much energy to it - it's probably just some stupid prank."

"Well, you know how I feel about pranks," Eliza said with a smirk.

"Oh, yes, I know how you feel about pranks," Susan laughed out loud. "Now, if you'll excuse me, it's time to go make a fresh pot of poison... I mean coffee."

The two friends laughed together, but as the laughter died down, that uneasy feeling had returned to Eliza's stomach. She hoped the police could figure out who sent that email, or at least set her mind at ease and blow it off as a prank, too. She also knew that she would be sure to spend some time that evening responding to that awful review.

But for now, she needed to finish this crust and get these quiches in the oven before the morning rush.

Chapter 3

Eliza curled up next to Dean on the couch, crossing her legs criss-cross applesauce style. She groaned as her leg muscles reminded her of her morning run. Pupcake jumped up next to her and then into her lap, settling in so that he was touching both Dean and Eliza.

"Can you see Dad, too, now?" Eliza asked, holding the phone out in front of her.

Laura laughed out loud. "Yes, Mom. Why do you always act like this is the first time you have ever had a FaceTime call?"

Eliza shrugged and laughed, "I'm old, Laura. I'm getting old."

"No you're not, Mom," Laura said. "You're not old, AND you are a business owner now! You're more than capable."

Eliza smiled at her daughter's beautiful face on the screen. "That's sweet, daughter," she said, "but tell me what you wanted to talk about."

"Oh, right. Hold on" Laura said. Eliza watched the screen as Laura carried the phone to shut her dorm room door. "Okay, are you ready for this?" She had her father's perfect smile.

"Yes!" Dean and Eliza responded with enthusiasm and in unison. Laura had their full attention, and Pupcake's, too. The little pup sat up straight, ears perked, watching the screen. Eliza had read that dogs couldn't see TV and phone screens like humans, but she wasn't convinced.

Laura took a deep breath, preparing to share her big news.

"I've met someone really special."

Eliza gasped and then squealed. "Oh my gosh! That's so exciting! Tell me everything!"

Dean sat quietly. He ran his hand through his hair. Eliza reached over and squeezed his knee. Dean took her hand into his, interlacing his fingers between hers.

"Well, his name is Carter Banks, and he's my same age," Laura began.

"Where is he from?" Eliza asked the first question.

"A small town in Louisiana," Laura responded. "His parents are still living there. He's an only child, so they're pretty close. His dad is a surgeon and his mother was a stay-at-home super mom like you, Mom."

Eliza noticed how Laura's face glowed when she talked about this new young man in her life.

"What is he studying?" Dean asked in what could only be described as a fatherly tone.

"Um, he's going for a double major. Communications and marketing," Laura said.

Eliza watched her husband's face. He looked either disappointed or concerned, she couldn't tell which.

"What does that look like for a career for him?" Eliza asked, hoping Laura would have an answer that would set Dean's mind at ease.

"So, he ultimately wants to be a YouTuber," Laura said, her smile had changed to a more forced smile, as if she had been apprehensive about this question and now dreaded the response to her answer. Then she quickly continued, "But, you know, Carter could do alot with that degree. He could work for a radio station, a. marketing firm... things like that."

"Oh, sure! No doubt that he could have a lot of opportunities with that. And a double major says he must have a lot of ambition," Eliza said, working hard to convince her husband and set Laura's nervousness at ease at the same time. Eliza wanted her daughter to be happy, and feel supported, no matter what.

Laura flashed a look of gratitude at the screen.

"Well, when do we get to meet this guy?" Dean asked. Laura had chosen to attend The University of Tennessee for her undergraduate degree, and her parents were relieved to have her stay close. The drive to the university from Copeland was a straight shot down the interstate less than two hours away.

"That's actually the other reason I was calling," Laura said. "We were thinking about heading in to see you two next weekend. Is that good with you?"

"Yes!," Eliza and Dean responded again the same, and practically in unison.

"Awesome! I can't wait for you to meet Carter. I'll reach out and see if Dalton is free, too," Laura said, referring to her older brother. Dalton was born two years, two months and two days before his sister, and although the two of them seemed to have a close relationship, Dalton couldn't be more different than his sister. He was always the quiet kid, his nose stuck in a book or inches away from a computer screen, but he was kind and thoughtful, like his father. In line with the overachiever that he was, Dalton had acquired a degree in electrical engineering in record time, finishing after less than three years, and had landed a government job where he seemed to always be working on important secret projects that he couldn't talk much about. Eliza doubted that he would be able to get away and join them, since he hardly even had time for a phone call whenever she reached out to him.

Before saying goodbye, Dean reminded Laura, "Hey, Laura, don't forget that your mom's big interview with the editor of the *Sugar and Spice* magazine is tomorrow."

"Oh, I haven't forgotten," Laura said with a wink. "How are you feeling about things, Mom?"

Eliza shifted the phone a bit to center herself in the frame. It was Eliza's turn to force a smile. "Mostly good," she responded. "Susan and I stayed later than normal today after closing to make sure everything is really clean. I would just die if the place didn't look perfect for pictures."

Laura nodded, her eyes sympathetic. "The place always looks really good. You don't have anything at all to worry about," Eliza's daughter assured her.

"Yeah, well, did you hear about the bad review we got?"

"No," Laura responded, confused.

"Well, someone put a review on Yelp and said my coffee tastes like poison."

"What?" Laura said. "I'm so shocked to hear that."

Eliza nodded. "Yeah, me too," she shrugged her shoulders and again put on a show that she hoped would convince both Laura and Dean of her indifference.

"You know that's not true, Mom."

"Yeah, I know," Eliza said, shifting the camera back to include both her and Dean, instantly regretting mentioning the review. She was surprised to find herself more emotional about it when telling Laura than she had been with telling Dean or Susan. She chalked it up to just feeling tired from the long, busy day.

"Well, it doesn't help that those people then turned around and emailed your mother some threatening message," Dean said.

Eliza squeezed Dean's hand and shot him a panicked look. She didn't want Laura to worry about her, and she had not intended on sharing the information about the email with her.

"What are you talking about? Who threatened you? I thought that sabotage stuff was behind you now," Laura's words flowed out of her mouth faster than a hummingbird's wings flutter about during flight.

Eliza recanted the whole story, catching Laura up on how Dean had visited the police earlier that day. Dean was assured by Chief Mason that there would be an investigation, and the chief of police offered to keep a close eye on things, as well.

"As far as I'm concerned," she shared with Dean and Laura, "the chief's response was encouraging. I'm not going to keep worrying about it."

"Sure, you're not," Laura teased her mom with a light tone. "Dad and I know you won't stop worrying about it, until you get to the bottom of it, but it's probably some stupid prank or misunderstanding of some kind. For now, hopefully you can just focus on tomorrow and enjoy that whole experience."

"I keep telling her this is what happens to celebrities," Dean jokes, winking at Eliza. "I mean, famous people get silly threats all the time from what I understand. She did win the county fair's baking competition after all. That kind of win changes your life." He lifted Eliza's hand to his mouth and kissed it. "I just know that I'm lucky you haven't left me, now that you have all this fame."

Eliza rolled her eyes, playing along with her husband's teasing.

"Yeah, all those crazy fans can be a lot to handle," Laura chimed in.

"Alright, alright," Eliza said. The three of them laughed together. "You two are awful!"

Dean and Laura grinned at each other through the phone screens.

"I have to go. I told Carter that I'd come over and watch a movie."

"Oh, okay. Go! We'll talk again soon," Eliza said. "Have fun tonight!"

"Bye, sweetpea!" Dean called out.

"Bye! Love you!" Laura responded.

"Love you, too," Eliza said and touched the red button on her phone to end the call.

She set her phone down on the coffee table and picked up Pupcake, lifting him to her face for a kiss. Eliza stretched out her legs and laid her head in Dean's lap, Pupcake on her chest.

"Seriously, dear, promise me you'll stop worrying about the email. There's nothing else we can do, and Joe basically said that it's harmless. I learned today that there's a term, keyboard warriors, that describes someone who is all talk behind their screen but otherwise harmless. He thinks that is most likely what we're dealing with," Dean said, as he stroked her hair away from her forehead.

Eliza looked up into her husband's beautiful eyes, nodded and smiled gratefully.

"I promise," she said quietly.

"Okay, good," Dean said. "Now, tell me about tomorrow. What's the plan?"

Eliza closed her eyes for a moment and took a deep breath before answering. Her thoughts drifted back to that wonderful day when she was awarded the blue ribbon for her popular strawberry cream cheese cupcakes at the county fair. She was shocked to find out that she had won the annual baking competition and was more than a little excited for The Pupcake Café to be featured in the renowned magazine. She opened the café less than a year ago and honestly had no expectations of this much success so quickly.

"Well, the *Sugar and Spice* team are expected to arrive at the café around ten o'clock tomorrow. That should work well, falling after the morning rush but before it gets crazy for lunch."

Dean continued slowly stroking his wife's hair as he listened.

"I have the strawberry cream cheese cupcakes ready, of course, but I also have my new lemon tart cupcakes that are really selling fast. So, I'm going to introduce those to them, as well, and see if they'll mention them in the article. But, really, I'm focusing on filling that case up with an array of different beautiful things and encouraging them to include a picture of that to show how much variety we have. Susan had a great idea of packing up our cute little go boxes full of goodies as gifts to give each member of their team."

Pupcake lifted his head and yawned, his tiny tongue rolling out as his mouth opened.

"Oh my gosh, you're so cute," Eliza said, distracted for a moment. She reached out and stroked Pupcake's cheek and he laid his head down and closed his eyes.

"But, now I'm thinking I need to make sure the coffee is perfect, too. That's probably the most stressful part of tomorrow. The last thing I need is for the editor of the *Sugar and Spice* magazine to think my coffee tastes like poison," Eliza said, only half-joking.

"Your coffee is delicious, Eliza," Dean said with a serious tone. "There is no way that fancy editor is going to say anything but wonderful things about you and The Pupcake Café."

"Oh my gosh, can you even imagine? I can just see it now," Eliza spreads her hands out as she continues, "a feature in *Sugar and Spice* magazine takes local coffee shop down with its review that confirms the coffee served at The Pupcake Café indeed tastes like poison." She covers her face with her hands and lets out a muffled groan.

Pupcake lifts his head and hurries to try to lick Eliza's face through her fingers.

"You're just being silly, now," Dean said, scooping Pupcake up in one of his large hands. "There's a reason you won that competition. And," he continued, stretching out the word for emphasis, "there's also a reason you have a morning rush and a lunch rush every single day."

Eliza uncovers her face and wiped the tear that hung onto the bottom lashes of her right eye. She hoped Dean didn't see it and produced a fake yawn to pretend that's why her eyes were watering.

Pupcake wiggled in Dean's hands trying desperately to get to Eliza so he could lick her face.

"Tomorrow is going to be wonderful, Eliza. Everything is going to go beautifully, and by the end of the day, you will have forgotten all about that stupid review."

Dean held Pupcake up by his face. "And besides, your two favorite guys will be there with you!"

Eliza smiled, sat up, and settled into Dean's lap. She wrapped her arms around both Dean and Pupcake.

"Group hug!" she said, chuckling. Burying her face in the crook where Dean's broad shoulder met his neck, she mumbled, "I just don't know how I could do any of this without the two of you."

"Well, the good news is that you don't have to," Dean said, pulling Eliza even closer to him.

"But, hang on, can we talk about this Carter guy now? A YouTuber? Is she serious?" Dean asked, playfully.

Eliza raised her head and laughed out loud.

"Don't worry, we'll give him the rundown when we meet him. And if we don't like him, we can just pour him a cup of our famous coffee," she said with a wink.

Chapter 4

Eliza glanced at the cute clock on the wall that displayed a drawing of cupcakes with a different color icing representing the different numbers. She took an intentional deep breath and let it out slowly, counting to seven. "Take a yoga breath," she remembered telling her kids when their stress levels seemed high, and this morning, she was taking her own advice.

The team from the *Sugar and Spice* magazine would be there in just a matter of hours, and Eliza felt like everything was going wrong.

The morning started with the toilet in the café's one bathroom needing to be fixed again. Eliza added a note to her task list to have a plumber come out and fix it for good.

Then, Susan got stuck in the walk-in cooler when the door's inside handle stuck. Thankfully, Eliza was right there to rescue her, but another fix-it task was added to the list. And from now on, they were to prop the door open each time they entered, for safety purposes.

While baking lemon tart cupcakes, Eliza discovered the ones she had stored in the walk-in cooler were not fresh, and were instead in quite bad shape. Susan being the life-saver that she was, offered to run to the store to grab some fresh lemons and Eliza took her up on the offer. But, now Eliza was starting to wonder what could be taking her friend so long. Her imagination was getting the best of her, picturing Susan broken down on the side of the road, and it didn't help matters that soon after Susan left, Eliza noticed she had left her phone on the upper shelf over the sink.

Eliza approached the back of the pastry case and decided to switch the placement of the cinnamon rolls with the jelly cookies, and walked around to the front of the case. She stood back to assess the change. Pupcake stood at her feet, looking up at his person, sensing her stress. Ignoring him, Eliza shook her head and returned to behind the counter, reached into the case and switched them back. She grabbed a cleaning towel and wiped a small smudge of icing that she spotted on the edge of the platter that held the strawberry cream cheese cupcakes, and then closed the case.

Pupcake pawed at the leg of her jeans. Eliza looked down to see him sitting with his back leg lifted, asking to be held. She knew he was just worried about her, but she didn't have time for Pupcake hugs right now.

"Mom's okay, Pupcake," Eliza said, realizing that she wasn't even able to convince herself. She needed to stay busy, and everything else but the lemon cupcakes was prepared. She decided to clean the dining area again while she waited, so she grabbed a towel from the bucket of bleach water and wrung it dry. For the second time that morning, she wiped all the tables and chairs down and inspected the individual flowers in their vases.

She glanced at the clock again. Ten more minutes had passed since she had last looked. She took another yoga breath before heading to the coffee station to make more coffee. She emptied the open bag of grounds into the filter and bent down to retrieve a new bag from the cabinet below, her mind, of course, jumping to that awful review again. She shuffled around in the cabinet looking for a new bag of coffee, pushing the bags of decaf to the side. She knew she had been low in stock, but she had specifically checked yesterday and thought that she surely had enough for a few more days.

Where in the world is it? Eliza thought to herself, feeling frantic. Pupcake was again by her feet. He leaned into her leg, remaining quiet, his big brown eyes focused on Eliza.

Eliza crumpled onto the floor, her back against the cabinet, her hands covering her face. Her shoulders moved in rhythm with her silent sobs.

I can't do this, she thought. *What was I even thinking opening a coffee shop at my age, with zero experience running a business? I'm just making a fool out of myself at this point.* Her thoughts continued, full of panic and worry.

Pupcake jumped in her lap and stretching his little legs as far as they could go, he propped his paws on either side of Eliza's neck. He licked the back of her hands and whimpered. Eliza uncovered her face and pulled Pupcake in close for a hug, her tears falling into the fur on the back of his neck as he rested his chin on her shoulder. Eliza wished she could just retreat to the safety of her home and cancel her day, but at that moment, Susan burst into the back door.

"I'm back, Eliza!" Susan called out, sounding a bit frantic herself. "Oh my gosh, it's when we need fresh lemons that they're the hardest to fi…" She stopped speaking when she spotted Eliza and Pupcake on the floor in front of the coffee station.

"Oh my gosh," Susan said for a second time. "You okay, Ellie?"

Eliza looked up at her friend and shook her head. Pupcake began licking the tears on her cheeks.

"We're out of coffee," she managed to say before a new set of tears emerged.

"No way," Susan said, and jumped into action, leaning down next to Eliza to inspect the cabinet. "Wait," she said, leaning back on her heels. "I'm going to go look in the back and see if maybe we just haven't put it away yet."

"Oh, that's right!" Eliza said, jumping to her feet. She remembered that there was a small unexpected delivery the day before during the morning rush. She had thrown it onto one of the empty shelves by the door and had totally forgotten about it until Susan mentioned it. The two headed back to investigate, fingers crossed that coffee was included in that order.

Opening the large box, Eliza pulled out kosher salt, paper napkins and a couple bags of stirring straws. There, at the bottom of the box, sat one ten pound bag of coffee grounds.

Eliza held the bag of precious coffee up in the air. "Woohoo!! We have coffee," she exclaimed, working to push her worries out of her mind and shift her mood.

"Yay!" Susan joined in, holding Pupcake in her arms. His tail wagged back and forth swiftly, and his mouth hung open in what could only be interpreted as a puppy grin.

"It's not the brand we usually have, and it's already ground" Eliza said, "but, we'll make it work." Looking back through the items in the box, Eliza continued, "Actually, I don't think I ordered any of this stuff."

"Oh, weird," Susan said, leaning over to look in the box, as well. "It must be the wrong order. It wasn't George who delivered it. It was some young kid. He said George was out sick or something and that he was covering for him."

"Well," Eliza shrugged. "At least we have enough to get through the morning. I can have Dean grab some more on his way into the shop."

"And now, you have the lemons, too," Susan said, setting Pupcake down and grabbing the bag of lemons she had brought with her.

"Thank you so much," Eliza said, inspecting the fruit. "These look beautiful." She headed right away to the sink where she scrubbed the lemons, dried them with paper towels, and carried them to the prepping station. As she began to lose herself in the baking process, she noticed her shoulders relaxing, pulling away from her ears. Sliding the pans of batter into the preheated oven, she glanced at the clock again. There was plenty of time left.

"Hey, you wanna try the new coffee?" Susan peeked her head around the corner from the front counter. "It's not bad!"

"Yes!" Eliza responded. "I'll be right there, and we can take a little break before we open." She set the finished frosting for the cupcakes aside and washed her hands.

Susan brought two cups of hot coffee back into the kitchen, and Eliza pulled two stools up to the prepping station.

"Are you feeling better, Ellie?" Susan asked carefully.

"Oh my gosh, yes," Eliza said with a smile. "Thank you for being such a good friend. I totally had a meltdown. I guess I'm more stressed out about the visit today than I thought I was."

"Well, you have already won the contest, so you have nothing to worry about, really," Susan said, pushing a small bowl of creamer towards Eliza's cup. "Everything is going to be fabulous."

"Yeah, I hope so," Eliza responded, pulling the creamer open and pouring it into her coffee. She stirred the coffee before taking a sip, eyes closed.

"What do you think?" Susan asked, referring to the coffee.

"Mm..." Eliza opened her eyes before responding, "I guess it's okay. It's definitely not as good, I don't think, but it will work."

"I think I might actually like it better. It has more of a nutty flavor than the other. What else do we need to do to get ready? Are you going to change clothes before they get here?"

Eliza nodded before taking another sip.

"Yeah, I'm going to change after the morning rush since there are going to be pictures and all. What about you?"

Before Susan could respond, there was a loud pounding at the back door. Pupcake came running, barking in his big boy voice. Eliza and Susan exchanged glances of confusion and stood to explore the situation together.

As they approached the door, Eliza called out, "Who is it?"

There was no answer. Pupcake continued barking, throwing his whole body into each yip.

"Should I open it?" Eliza whispered to Susan. Susan shook her head. Eliza looked back at the door, wishing she had a peephole like on her front door at home. She had an idea. "I'm going to go out the front door and peek around the side of the building and see if anyone is there. Don't move."

Another loud pounding on the door made both women jump and Susan grabbed Eliza's arm. Pupcake added snarls in with his barks, lunging at the door, the tiny hairs on his back standing on end.

"Who is it?" Eliza called out again, trying desperately to hide her fear from her voice.

A man's voice mumbled something indecipherable. Eliza and Susan both looked at each other, shook their heads and shrugged their shoulders as if in agreement that neither knew what he said.

"We're closed!" Eliza called out sternly.

"Should I call 911?" Eliza whispered to Susan. "We're opening in twenty minutes."

"I don't know," Susan whispered back. "Maybe he left?"

"Okay, I'm going out the front to look," Eliza said. "Keep an eye on Pupcake, and do not open this door." Eliza approached the front door, looking both ways as far as she could see down the street. Nothing seemed out of place or unusual. She watched as a young couple entered the diner down the street and as a man dressed in a suit slid into the driver's seat of his Mercedes. She unlocked the door and slipped out, turning toward the end of the building to get a good view of the small private lot. She peeked around the corner, her heart beating out of her chest. There was no one to be found, but she could see a box sitting outside the back door of the café.

She turned to head back into the front door to report to Susan what she saw. Turning, Eliza found herself suddenly face to face with Mr. Stewart. A squeal escaped her lips and she instinctively pushed him away. The elderly man grabbed onto the wall to keep his balance.

"Oh, Mr. Stewart!" She exclaimed. "I'm so sorry! You scared me!"

Mr. Stewart grumbled something incoherent and hustled past her, his hands rolled into fists. Eliza instantly felt terrible for pushing him and was glad she didn't knock him off his feet. Everyone in Copeland knew Mr. Stewart as the grouchy old man in town. He had lived there his whole life, and just was never very friendly with anyone. She was always curious about his life, but no one she knew ever had any clue about his story.

Susan popped her head out of the door, holding Pupcake in her arm like a football.

"Are you okay, Ellie? I heard you scream," her tone quickly turned from concern to a scolding. "You scared me to death!"

"I'm fine," Eliza said, grabbing the door from Susan, entering and locking up behind her. She told her about how she almost knocked over Mr. Stewart.

"We only have about ten minutes left until we open now," she announced, glancing again at the clock on the way to the backdoor. "And there's a package at the back door. I guess maybe that was just a delivery guy earlier."

Eliza unlocked the heavy door and pulled it open. There sat the package she saw from the front of the building. On it was a handwritten note that read, *A special gift for your big day.*

Susan peered over her shoulder and read the note aloud. "I wonder who it's from," she asked the question that was also on Eliza's mind.

Eliza pulled the box inside and shut the door, locking it again. She pulled off the note to get a closer look. It looked like a normal piece of printer paper. The writing was in red ink and almost child-like handwriting. Eliza wasn't sure why she found that odd, but she was suddenly worried about opening the box.

"Something's not right, Susan," Eliza said. "I'm going to have Dean open this when he comes in this morning. We need to go and start our day anyway."

"Yeah, good plan," Susan said, as the two women stared at the mystery box on the floor and watched as Pupcake walked around sniffing every inch of the package. His tail was straight up in the air and a high pitched, but quiet, whine could be heard during his examination.

It was clear that Pupcake also did not trust what was in the box.

Chapter 5

Eliza instantly felt a sense of relief when she saw her handsome husband, Dean, walk through the front door of The Pupcake Café. Just as quick as he entered, he stepped right back out to hold the door open for a small group of older women who had just finished their breakfast. The ladies thanked Dean as they walked past him, and he wished them a beautiful day.

Eliza met Dean halfway in the dining area and gave him a big hug.

"Thanks for coming, love. I'm a nervous wreck."

"I wouldn't miss it for the world. I'm just glad I could get away. For a minute, I was worried I would be late, but things came together just fine."

"Sounds like you're having a similar morning, then," Eliza said, running her hand down his arm to grab his hand.

"Everything okay?" Dean asked, looking around. Pupcake was sitting in front of Dean, his back leg lifted. Dean released Eliza's hand and bent down to scoop up the pup. "How are you holdin' up, little guy?" Dean asked, and Pupcake responded with lots of kisses.

Eliza couldn't wait to tell Dean everything, but one quick glance at the clock told her that the magazine crew would be there anytime.

"The morning has been crazy. The toilet broke again, and now the walk-in cooler door isn't opening from the inside. You know, just the normal stuff that happens when you own a coffee shop and are being interviewed and photographed later that day." Eliza chuckled, trying to make light of it all, but she was extremely nervous and sure that she couldn't hide that from Dean.

Dean set Pupcake down and grabbed Eliza's hand. He glanced at his watch.

"Let's see, if they're on time, they'll be here in about five minutes. Chances are they won't be on time, though. I've heard that about magazine crews," he joked.

Eliza couldn't help but giggle.

"And you look amazing, honey," Dean continued. "You sure hide the sweat well. I would never even know you were nervous, so just remember to be your confident self, and you'll do totally fine."

Susan came around the corner from the kitchen.

"Hi, Dean! It's great to see you! Your superstar wife here has us all ready for this big event."

"I see that," Dean said, looking around. "Did y'all chase the people out or something?" He winked at Eliza.

"Nah, we're typically empty right around this time. That's the way I wanted it for the interview," Eliza responded, tucking her hair behind her ear. It was weird wearing her hair down in the café. She always had it up in a ponytail when she was working.

"Oh! Don't forget about the package in the back," Susan reminded Eliza.

"A package?" Dean asked, raising his eyebrows.

"Yeah," Eliza responded, pulling him toward the kitchen. "I'll have to tell you more about it, but we got a strange package I would love for you to open."

Before they could walk past the front counter, the chime on the front door sounded and Sharon McArthur, the editor of the *Sugar and Spice* magazine, walked in wearing a big friendly smile. Eliza turned on her heels and rushed to greet her.

"Hi, Sharon! Welcome to The Pupcake Café!"

"Hi, Eliza! Oh my gosh, this place is the best! It's so cute!" Pupcake ran up to Sharon and gently pawed at her bare ankles. Dean swooped in and scooped him up.

"Hi, Sharon, it's great to see you again," Dean said, reaching out his arm to shake her hand. "Dean Campbell, lucky husband to the star, and you probably remember Pupcake more than you'd remember me." He motioned to Pupcake as if introducing royalty.

Sharon laughed out loud. "Oh, I remember you both!" She leaned in to let Pupcake give her a quick kiss on the cheek. "Hi, sweet thing," she said, in a stronger Southern accent than Eliza had remembered. She had read that the office of the magazine was in Chicago, and she wondered what brought the Stillson County Fair to their attention.

Turning to Susan, Eliza motioned for her to join them.

"Sharon, I'd like to introduce my friend - and now co-worker - Susan Morris. Susan, this is Sharon McArthur."

"It's a real pleasure to meet you," Susan said. "I've been a huge fan of the magazine for years."

"The pleasure is mine," Sharon said, and Eliza noticed the Southern accent had again disappeared.

"Is this your first time in Copeland?" Susan asked.

"Oh, no," Sharon replied. "I actually grew up not far from here in a very small town, aptly named Smallville."

"Interesting," Dean said. "Do you happen to know Clark Kent?"

The group shared a laugh.

"Funny, I get asked that a lot," Sharon said with a chuckle. "But no. There was only one Superman in that town, and it was my father."

The door chime rang again and two men entered in single file. One was carrying a large light on a stand and the other was carrying what looked like an electrical box of some kind with a big bag thrown over his shoulder.

Right behind them, a couple entered and approached the counter. Then, just a couple seconds later, a middle-aged man entered and stood in line behind the couple.

"Oh! I should get to work," Susan said, heading back behind the counter.

The door chime rang again and three women in either their late twenties or early thirties rambled into the shop and stood in line.

"Well, so much for a quiet moment," Eliza said, apologetically.

Sharon waved her hand in the air as if to dismiss the apology.

"No, this is what we want to capture," she assured Eliza. "Please go about your day and we'll get set up. We will start with some random photos, and then I'll pull you away for the interview and more pictures."

Eliza agreed, but she felt uneasy about ignoring her special guest. She joined Susan behind the counter, but Susan insisted she could handle the small crowd.

"Go, open the package," Susan said. "I'm dying to see what's in it!"

Eliza nodded and asked Dean to join her in the back for a quick minute. He was holding Pupcake and chatting with one of the crew members, but he excused himself.

"What is happening with this box?" Dean asked. "Is there a reason you're waiting for me to open it?"

"Yes," Eliza insisted. "I haven't had a chance to tell you everything, but it was left at the back door with this note." She showed her husband the note and stood patiently as he read it. Like Eliza, Dean turned it over to inspect the back.

"That's weird," Dean said.

"Agreed. I had a really weird feeling about it, so I decided to wait for you."

Dean passed Pupcake off to Eliza and tore the tape off the box. He opened the flaps to reveal an assortment of little gifts. Right on top was a bag containing individual packets of different flavors of sugar. Eliza picked it up and examined it. She saw little clear packets of sugar in several different flavors: banana, hibiscus, cinnamon, cranberry, lavender, ginger, maple, and more.

"Ooooh, that's so interesting," Eliza said. "I guess people can add this to their tea."

"Or their coffee if they wanted to," Dean said.

"True," Eliza leaned over to see what else was in the box. She found what was clearly a used coffee table book with pictures taken all over beautiful sights in Tennessee. The pages were yellowed and the cover was creased.

Next, Eliza pulled out two simple white coffee mugs. "So strange," Eliza pondered. "Who do you think sent this?"

"I have no idea," Dean said. "There's no card, no address on the box anywhere. It is someone local here, I would guess." He pulled out the last gift in the box, a small square box and opened it to find a red leather dog collar bedazzled with tiny different colored stones.

"Oh, that's so cute!" Eliza exclaimed. She took the box and collar and placed Pupcake in Dean's arms. She slipped the collar onto Pupcake's neck and fastened it. He growled in protest. "Now, now, Pupcake," Eliza said in her typical mom voice, "I left it loose so that you wouldn't really feel it that much."

Pupcake wiggled as if to say he wanted down and Dean set him down on the floor. He immediately went into scratching mode, trying to get the collar off of his neck.

"You look so cute," Susan said from behind Eliza. "So, this is the box, huh?" She asked, leafing through the book. "Was there a note? Do you know who it's from?"

Eliza shook her head. "No, there was no note."

"Well, it was a nice gesture, all the same," Susan said, examining the sugar packets. "Want me to go put these on the coffee station?" she asked.

"Yes, please do," Eliza replied. "Which reminds me, I didn't even offer Sharon and the crew anything to drink!"

"Oh, I did," Susan said. "They're fixing their cups now, actually."

"Oh perfect," Eliza said. "I'll get back out there and see if we can get this interview process started then."

They all returned to the front. The three young women had taken their coffees to go, but the couple and the male customer were all seated with their drinks. The man was preoccupied with his phone, and the couple appeared to be on a date, holding hands across the table, in deep conversation. The door chime rang and one of their beloved regular customers, Mrs. Wilson, entered the shop.

"Hi, Eliza!" Mrs. Wilson called out.

Eliza instantly wondered if the gift was from her.

"Hi, Mrs. Wilson! It's good to see you! How was your Florida trip?" She debated silently how to ask the question if she was the gift sender.

"It was beautiful and sunny, but I'll tell you what. It's so good to be back! I have missed your coffee!"

"Well, it's good to have you back. We've missed seeing you," Eliza said sincerely. Mrs. Wilson was one of her very best customers, spreading the word all around town about The Pupcake Café.

Eliza saw Susan spreading out the little packets of sugar on display on the coffee stand, Sharon standing next to her admiring the choices. She could hear Sharon squeal with joy when she spotted the cranberry sugar.

"Oh my gosh, I absolutely love cranberry sugar!" Sharon said. "I haven't had that since I was a kid, but I used to be obsessed with it."

"Well, you should take it then," Susan said. "I imagine that might taste pretty good in your coffee. And there's only one of those, so it's yours." Eliza watched as Susan opened the small packet and poured it into Sharon's cup.

Sharon thanked Susan and proceeded to stir her coffee. "So, you don't always have these sugar choices?" She asked. "I hate to take your last cranberry sugar."

"No, we don't typically have flavored sugar. We just got these as an anonymous gift, but you're more than welcome to have that one. And maybe I can convince Eliza to order some for regular stock going forward."

Eliza shifted her attention back to Mrs. Wilson. "So, what can I get you today? The same order as you always got before, or do you like something different now that you've been away for so long?" Eliza smiled.

"Oh honey, I'll take my usual," Mrs. Wilson replied.

Eliza nodded and turned to make Mrs. Wilson's chai latté. With one hand on the steam valve knob, she glanced over to see Dean back in conversation with the crew. Pupcake was napping in his bed, right at their feet.

Finishing Mrs. Wilson's drink order, Eliza turned to collect her customer's favorite cheese danish from the dish, moving the other danishes to hide an empty spot on the platter. She boxed it up for her and set it on the counter next to her drink.

One of the crew members swooped in and took a photo of the cup and box on the counter.

Mrs. Wilson just ignored the photographer next to her and began looking around in her purse for something. Eliza assumed she was looking for change, and she assured her, like she did every day, that her order was on the house. And like every other day, Mrs. Wilson pushed back gently with a "you don't have to do that." It's a dance Eliza had become familiar with, and always knew it would end with Mrs. Wilson dropping a five dollar bill in the tip jar.

But, this time, before she dropped the tip, Mrs. Wilson leaned in and whispered, "Honey, did you happen to see that Yelp review someone posted? It's horrible... just horrible. I can't imagine anyone saying anything like that about this place."

Eliza felt a pit in her stomach. None of her customers had mentioned it to her yet and she had hoped that no one would actually see it.

Before Eliza could answer, however, a commotion of some kind erupted by where Dean and the crew were seated. Sharon had joined them with her coffee cup in hand. Eliza heard her start coughing and looked over to see concerned expressions on the faces of the photographer, the other crew member, and Dean. Pupcake barked and kept looking back and forth between Eliza and Sharon as if he were trying to tell Eliza something.

"One second, Mrs. Wilson," Eliza said, quickly heading over to see what was happening. Her ceramic coffee mug fell to the ground with a crash. Pupcake jumped and took cover under the closest table, barking incessantly. Eliza watched in horror as Sharon continued to gasp for air, clawing at her throat.

"Sharon!" Eliza called out, "Are you okay?" Eliza grabbed Sharon's arm and pounded her back, but Sharon wiggled out of her grasp, falling to her knees, still clutching her neck. The coughing had subsided and she was silent. The color in her face faded to a pale white.

Dean and Eliza both dropped to their knees next to Sharon, holding onto her arms to keep her upright. Eliza felt completely helpless.

"Was she eating something?" Eliza screamed. "Dean, should we do the Heimlich?"

Dean jumped into action and wriggled behind Sharon, wrapping his arms around her waist. He pulled her body close into his with quick jolts using his fists, but her body went limp.

"Call 911!" Eliza screamed. "Call 911!"

The two men in the crew stood in shock as they watched the scene. Mrs. Wilson stood at the counter as a spectator as well, scared and motionless. The couple still sitting at the table nearby mimicked the same, their mouths open and eyes wide.

Eliza saw the bathroom door fly open. Susan came running, her apron untied, loose, and hanging on her neck.

"What's happening?" Susan cried out, kneeling down beside Eliza.

Tears streamed down Eliza's face. "Call 911," she repeated, before she realized the young man who was there on a date was already on the phone with a dispatcher.

"The ambulance is on the way," he said, his face flushed and remaining on the line with them. The young woman sat frozen in her seat next to him.

"Please go find Pupcake," Eliza said to Susan, as she continued to hold onto Sharon's lifeless arm. Susan nodded and collected Pupcake from under the table. He had stopped barking, but just like his owner, he was trembling all over. Susan carried him to the front door and flipped the open sign to closed.

Dean had laid Sharon's body down carefully and he leaned over her, feeling for a pulse. Realizing just how serious the situation had become, he wrapped his arms around Eliza and slowly rocked her back and forth.

"It's going to be okay," he said over and over again... but Eliza knew the truth.

Nothing was okay.

Chapter 6

The ambulance was the first to arrive, but Chief Joe Mason was only minutes behind them. Sharon was pronounced dead on the scene, and the coroner was called to collect her body.

The photographer, whose name Eliza finally learned was Steve, was crying as the first responders carefully moved her body onto a gurney and wheeled her out the door. The other crew member, whose name Eliza had yet to learn, was sitting on the floor in the corner of the dining area, his arms wrapped around his knees. He had a vacant stare as he watched the scene unfold.

Mrs. Wilson sat at one of the smaller tables with Chief Mason. She had a hair appointment and asked if she could be the first to be questioned so she could leave.

Susan had brought Pupcake to Eliza and Dean, who sat in silence at one of the larger tables. The young couple sat huddled at their table nearby. Susan was leaning against the wall by the restroom with her arms crossed, chewing on her lip.

Mrs. Wilson was excused to go, and before she left she approached Eliza to give her a hug. Eliza sat motionless, in shock over what had just happened.

"I'm so sorry, Eliza," Mrs. Wilson said. "It will be okay. Everything will be okay."

Why does everyone keep saying that? Eliza thought to herself. *Someone just died right here in my café. And not just someone, but Sharon McArthur! How is everything going to be okay?*

Mrs. Wilson gave Eliza one more quick squeeze and then waved to Susan before heading out the door with her latte and danish in hand.

Chief Mason approached Eliza and Dean and explained that he would talk to the other customers next. Dean nodded and said that was fine. Eliza wanted desperately just to go home. She looked at Dean and knew he felt the same. Dean scooted his chair closer and put his arm around Eliza. She leaned the side of her face into his chest and held Pupcake close to hers.

Susan came over to where Eliza and Dean were sitting and asked quietly, "Can I get you guys anything? Eliza, when was the last time you ate something?"

"I'm not hungry," Eliza replied, tears welling up in her eyes again.

Dean answered, "Thank you, Susan. I think a couple cups of green tea would be good."

Susan nodded with a look of gratitude and sped off to fill the request.

Eliza could overhear Chief Mason say, "Okay, thank you both for your patience. I think we have all we need from you today. I have your contact information, so if anything else comes up, I'll be in touch."

The couple thanked him and gathered their things. The woman stopped in her tracks just in front of the door and said, "I'm not sure we paid for our coffee."

Eliza heard the young man say, "It's fine. I think that might be the least of their worries right now." He grabbed her hand and led her on their way and the chief locked the door behind them.

Steve, the photographer, had managed to cross the room and sit next to his fellow unnamed crew member without Eliza realizing it. Chief Mason made his way over to the two of them and pulled up a chair. She watched as Steve both consoled the shocked man and coherently answered Chief Mason's questions at the same time.

Susan appeared and set two cups of tea on the table in front of them.

"Thank you, Susan," Dean said quietly, his voice sounded like he was fighting a cold, but Eliza knew it was a result of a runny nose turned stuffy after crying.

"Thank you, Susan," Eliza muttered. "Why don't you sit down?"

Susan seemed grateful for the invitation. She pulled a chair up to the table and sat on the edge, fidgeting with the cuticles on her short fingernails.

"My instinct is to clean, but Joe told me not to touch anything," she said.

Eliza nodded, sitting straight in her chair and taking a sip of the tea.

"Mmmm...the tea helps a little," Eliza said.

"I thought it would. You should probably eat something too, Ellie," Susan said. "What about you, Dean? I'm happy to cook something if y'all want it."

"I don't think my stomach could handle it," Eliza said, "but thank you."

"I'm fine, too, for now," Dean said. "Hopefully we'll get to go home soon." He reached over and petted Pupcake. Pupcake jumped and trembled a little bit at the touch.

"He probably needs to go potty," Eliza said. She rose to her feet and started moving toward the front door. There was a small grassy area out front that Pupcake was familiar with. As she reached for the door, Chief Mason turned in his seat.

"Eliza," he said firmly. "You can't leave."

Eliza stopped and turned toward the police chief.

"I'm not..." she uttered the only two words she could think and then shot a helpless look at Dean.

"She's just taking Pupcake out to go to the bathroom," Dean said, jumping to his feet.

"Hang on, then," the chief said. He mumbled something into his radio and a young officer appeared outside the front door. "Officer Crump will escort you out there."

Eliza looked toward Dean again for support.

Dean walked over to her, and said, "I'll go with you."

Chief Mason interjected, also standing, "No. Just one of you needs to go."

Dean's face turned red and his brow furrowed. "What are you..." His words trailed off as he quickly regained his composure. He turned back to Eliza. "Here let me take him," he said, reaching to collect Pupcake from Eliza's arms. Pupcake leaned into Eliza and looked at Dean with wide frightened eyes.

"No, it's okay, Dean," Eliza said. "I'll do it. I'll be right back. We're just going like five feet away."

"Okay," Dean said softly and he unlocked the door and held it open for his wife. He stood in the doorway and watched until they returned.

Eliza, Dean and Pupcake settled back into their seats at the table with Susan. The breath of fresh air brought some calm to Eliza but her mind was spinning for answers on what just happened.

"Susan," Eliza whispered. "Did Sharon eat anything?" It definitely looked to her as if Sharon had choked on something.

Susan shook her head. "No, not that I know of. She only had coffee," she whispered back. "What even happened? I mean, I went to the restroom and then I heard the crash of the cup being dropped and you screaming to call 911."

"That's basically all we know, too," Dean whispered. "She came over raving about how delicious her coffee was when just all of a sudden, she started choking."

"Wait. Can someone choke on coffee?" Eliza whispered. *Please, god, no,* Eliza thought. If Sharon died because she choked on her coffee, there would be no recovering from that as a coffee shop.

Susan stared blankly at Eliza. "I don't know," she said, as if she didn't know what else to say.

Eliza watched as Chief Mason wrapped up the conversation with the two men in the crew. He turned and approached their table and requested to speak with Susan alone next. She joined him at a table across the room. Steve and the other crew member began gathering their things. The other crew member hung his head as he carried the large light out the door. Before leaving, Steve stopped to say goodbye.

"I don't know what to say," he began, "but it was nice to meet both of you." He reached out his arm to shake hands with Dean and offered a handshake to Eliza, as well. She lightly touched his hand and thanked him for coming.

"Is your coworker okay?" Eliza asked.

"He will be," Steve said. "He and Sharon had worked together for a few years, so it's going to be hard to say goodbye."

"We're so sorry for your loss," Dean said, empathetically. "I wish we could have done more."

"As far as I'm concerned, you did all you could," Steve said. "No one knows why these things happen, but you're good people, and so was she." He cast his eyes down to the floor.

"I don't know what will happen next with the feature in the magazine," he went on to explain. "I guess they'll be in touch to reschedule. I did get some photos we could use, but I'm aware that the interview never happened."

"Oh, please don't even worry about that," Eliza said. She wasn't even sure if she would still be in business after this.

"Oh!" Steve said, remembering something. He set the bag on the floor and rifled through it, pulling out the latest episode of the *Sugar and Spice* magazine. "Sharon was going to give this to you. She had asked me to help her remember to leave it with you before she left." He placed it on the table in front of them.

"Thank you," Eliza said. "Have a safe flight home." As soon as the words escaped her lips, she realized the gravity of that saying and tears began to emerge on her bottom lashes again.

"Yes," Dean said. "Thank you." He stood to shake his hand properly and walked him to the door, locking it behind him as Chief Mason watched him from across the room.

The room was quiet now with only Eliza, Dean and Pupcake at one table and Susan and Chief Mason at another. It felt to Eliza like Chief Mason was trying to keep things in a hushed tone, which made her want to listen even more. Dean settled back in his chair and leaned over to whisper to Eliza.

"Steve is such a cool..." Eliza held her finger up to stop him talking so she could eavesdrop on the conversation happening across the room.

"Well, yes, just coffee," she could hear Susan say.

"She didn't use creamer, only sugar," again, Eliza could only hear Susan's answers and not the chief's questions.

"Um, no, it was actually cranberry sugar." Eliza heard Susan gasp, and she leaned further in their direction. "Maybe she was allergic to cranberries!" Susan sounded as if she had solved a crime, but then she quickly changed her tone as another thought crossed her mind. "But, no, she actually said she was obsessed with cranberry sugar when she was younger. So, she couldn't have been allergic... unless maybe she developed an allergy over the years...?" Susan was just rambling, thinking out loud at this point, and it was making Eliza uncomfortable. For the first time, she was realizing the gravity of this happening in The Pupcake Café. She knew how fast rumors could fly in the small town of Copeland, and she felt as if she was watching her dreams slip right down the drain.

Dean reached out and squeezed Eliza's hand.

"Honey, please try not to worry," he said, as if he could read her mind. "Things have a way of working themselves out."

Eliza nodded, blinking away tears and wishing the pit in her stomach would just go away for good.

She wanted to believe Dean, but she worried that after today, she would have an insurmountable hill to climb to save the café.

Chapter 7

Eliza rolled over on her side in bed and pulled the covers over her head, shutting out the sunlight streaming in through the open curtains. She felt around for Pupcake and found him lying on Dean's pillow next to hers. She began petting him when he stood, stretched long starting from his neck and pushing all the way through his tail. He sauntered sleepily to get closer to Eliza, crawled under the covers and laid down right next to her, rolling onto his back for a belly rub.

Dean was sitting in the chair by the window and startled Eliza when he spoke. "Honey, you should get up. It has been three days, and I'm starting to get worried about you."

Eliza groaned and remained under the covers, fighting back tears again.

"Susan came by to see you earlier. She's worried, too."

Eliza remained silent. All she wanted to do was sleep.

"Why don't you just get up and take a shower?" Dean persisted.

"I can't, Dean," Eliza replied meekly.

Dean crawled into bed behind Eliza and held her.

"How about you just go lay on the couch for a change?" Dean asked quietly.

"It's too bright in the living room," Eliza said.

They laid in silence for a long few minutes before Dean spoke again.

"You're going to have to get out of bed some time, Eliza. It's not ever going to be easy, but you have to do it. You have people that love you and are concerned about you. Laura has called several times a day. She's anxious to talk to you. She's coming home tomorrow."

Eliza felt dread creep under her skin. "How am I going to face Laura when I can't even stop crying, Dean?" Then, remembering the weekend plans, she said, "She's not bringing her new boyfriend, is she?"

"No," Dean said. "She's smart enough to know that's not a good idea right now."

"Dalton has been calling, too. He's going to try and get away from work to come into town, too, now."

"Ugghhh..." Eliza groaned longer and louder this time, throwing the covers off of her. "Fine. I'll take a shower."

Dean sat up and let out a sigh of relief.

Pupcake curled into a cute little ball, snuggling up closer now that the covers weren't there.

Eliza sat up, but she kept her eyes cast down. A tear escaped the eyelashes on her right eye and she quickly wiped it away. Another followed right after, tracing the path that the previous tears had left behind.

"It's okay to cry, honey," Dean said. "But maybe you should go see Doctor Richards. I feel like he might be able to give you something just temporarily..."

Eliza didn't respond. She knew Dean was worried, but for whatever reason, the suggestion to get on medications felt hurtful. She slipped her feet out from under the covers and placed them on the floor. With the exception of a bathroom break here and there, Dean was right, she had been in bed too long. Her body felt stiff and old.

"I'm going to take a shower, Dean," she repeated, as she stood to walk to the bathroom, straightening her nightshirt that had become twisted around her waist.

"I'm proud of you, honey!" Dean called out, as she shut the door and turned the water on its hottest setting. She knew she had no reason to be angry or even annoyed at Dean. He was trying to hold everything together for her, just like he did when Laura, her youngest and last child to move out, left home for college.

It took all the energy she had to stand up from the toilet and step into the shower. She felt dizzy after days with little to no nutrients, so she sat, naked, on the floor of the tub. She hugged her knees, letting the lukewarm water hit the top of her head and roll down her back. She closed her eyes and felt the water get warmer as she replayed in her mind every detail about the last few seconds of Sharon McArthur's life. The tears rolled down her face and she lifted her face toward the stream of water, allowing the shower to wash them away as quickly as they escaped.

It felt like an eternity, but Eliza somehow finally reached the point where she thought there might be no tears left. She crawled onto her hands and feet and then held onto the side of the tub as she slowly and carefully rose to her feet. She grabbed her loofah and squirted body wash into it then watched in what felt like slow motion as she scrubbed her skin, beginning with her arms.

Dean was right. She needed a shower. She needed to feel like she could wash off all the terrible stuff that had happened just a few days ago. She needed to cleanse her soul, her memories, and a shower was the closest thing to that.

After washing and rinsing her hair, Eliza stepped out of the shower to find a warm towel, and a clean shirt, under-wear and yoga pants on the counter. How did she not even see Dean pop in there with those surprises, she wondered to herself. She wrapped the oversized towel around tired body and sat on the edge of the tub.

Dean knocked quietly on the door. "Everything okay in there, Eliza?" he asked softly.

"Yes, thank you for the towel and clothes, love," Eliza said, and even she surprised herself with how much stronger she sounded. "I'll be right out."

After applying lotion and moisturizer, getting dressed and combing her wet hair, Eliza emerged from the bathroom a new person. Dean sat in the chair by the window and Eliza could see a sense of relief wash over his face.

"I made some soup," he said. "Want to come to the kitchen to eat?"

Eliza nodded and scooped Pupcake out of the bed to join them.

Settling into their designated dining room chairs across from each other, with Pupcake curled up in the chair next to her, Eliza felt assured that things could feel normal again. Dean had placed a bowl of minestrone soup on the table in front of her, a black and gray checkered cloth napkin and a soup spoon laid next to it. Dean had a tendency to collect kitchen gadgets, and she remembered the day he brought home the hard plastic soup spoons from the store. He was as excited as a little boy to show her how he had run across these spoons, "just like the ones they use in Chinese restaurants when they serve your favorite egg drop soup! I had to get them!" Even though she teased him at the time, Eliza could admit he was right. It was indeed nice to have soup spoons as an addition to their collection of silverware.

She picked up the spoon and scooped a mixture of vegetables, pasta and tomato base. She inhaled the aroma before taking a sip. "Mmmm.... the soup is good, love." She cast a grateful smile his way. "Thank you for taking such good care of me. I'm sorry I'm such a mess."

Dean reached across the table and squeezed her hand. He said three simple words, his eyes locked with hers. "I love you, Eliza."

"I love you, too," she replied, grateful that she wasn't again having to fight tears. Maybe the shower truly did help her wash away the intense sadness and fear she was experiencing. She could only hope that was the case. She didn't want to worry her kids when they visited any more than she already had.

"So, have I missed anything from the past few days?" Eliza asked.

Dean leaned back in his chair, exhaling a controlled breath. "Well, Laura is married now, and Dalton just bought a mansion in Dubai. Pupcake even got another chihuahua pregnant, so I've been dealing with that."

Eliza almost spit her soup back into her bowl to keep from choking on it as she laughed at Dean's updates. Carefully swallowing the soup in her mouth, she regained her composure, and laughed out loud.

"Oh my god, Dean. You're hilarious." She shook her head, but the smile stayed in place for a few minutes longer.

"What?" Dean continued with the joke, "You think I'm kidding? You've been asleep forever. The world doesn't just stop spinning because you're asleep, you know."

Eliza set her spoon down in the half empty bowl and cocked her head. Her smile turned into a closed lip grin. "Seriously, though, any real news?"

Dean shook his head, his arms crossed. "What are you wanting to hear, honey? We live in the small town of Copeland. Not a lot happens in just three days. Maybe the kids will have real news when they come to visit tomorrow."

Eliza leaned forward and swallowed another spoonful of delicious vegetables and pasta. "Your minestrone is the best, Dean, for real. It's so good."

"Well, I made enough to feed an army, so eat up."

Eliza swallowed another spoonful before summoning the courage to ask the question she really wanted the answer to: "Have you heard from Chief Mason?" She averted her eyes and looked into her bowl of soup.

"I did talk to him earlier today for just a few minutes," Dean said. "Are you sure you want to talk about this, though?"

Eliza lifted her eyes to meet his. "Yes, of course. Why? Is there a reason I shouldn't want to talk about this?"

"Well, no," Dean said. "I just don't want to dwell on what happened if you're feeling better."

"I can't pretend it didn't happen, Dean. I don't need Doctor Richards to tell me that's not healthy."

"Right," Dean said. "Okay. All Joe basically said was that they are still waiting on the toxicology report results to announce the cause of death. I guess her most current medical records don't show any obvious natural causes. And her family is now pretty involved and wanting to find out what happened."

Dean was right. Eliza suddenly felt like she needed to vomit. She took a long drink of her water and tried to hide the panic she was feeling from the one who knew her the best. Something told her that this wasn't going to go away easily. She worried for the future of her beloved coffee shop.

Suddenly, she wasn't hungry any more, so she pushed her nearly empty bowl towards the center of the table. She leaned on her elbows in front of her, her mind searching for the next thing to say.

"Hm," she mumbled. "I bet her family is just broken-hearted. She seemed so kind. And young. She was way too young to..." Eliza left off the last word.

She began folding and refolding her cloth napkin, pressing the edges with the tip of her finger, lost in thought.

"She said she grew up close to here. I wonder if we're expected to attend the funeral," Eliza said, keeping her eyes focused on the napkin.

Dean sat quietly, studying his wife's face.

"I mean, how do you Google something like that?" Eliza tried to make light of the situation and make her own joke, but Dean didn't laugh.

"I don't think we knew her well enough to attend her funeral," Dean said slowly and carefully.

"Right," Eliza responded, nodding. "Right."

After a pause, she continued, "But I mean, how well," she held two fingers up to mimic air quotes, "do you have to know someone to be there when they take their last breath. Does that not constitute knowing someone well enough to attend their funeral?"

Dean sat silent and pensive before answering. "I think I'm just wondering why you would want to attend her funeral."

Eliza pushed her chair away from the table and stood up, gathering her bowl and spoon in her hands. "Yeah, you're right. I will admit I have no idea how to navigate any of this. I've never even witnessed a pet die, let alone a person. But you're right, we're certainly not expected to attend her funeral. I guess I'm just bracing myself for the small town rumors that must be circling right now. Are they going to think I'm cold and heartless if I don't go? Or can I even control any of that?"

She sat back down on the chair, harder than she expected, setting the dishes back on the table. All of a sudden, she felt super tired again.

Dean rose to his feet and reached down to hug Eliza, slipping his arms under her armpits and lifting her to her feet. He hugged her, supporting her weight and almost lifting her off the ground.

"Let's go sit on the couch for a while," he whispered in her ear and kissed her neck.

"Okay," Eliza agreed meekly, and she let Dean help her walk to where she would normally sit when they watched television together or just hung out and chatted. She clicked her tongue to call Pupcake, and he came running, curling up in her lap after reaching up for a quick kiss. She sat criss-cross applesauce style with her back against the arm of the couch and stroked Pupcake's fur along his back.

Dean cleared the table and brought Eliza her water. "How about a game of Rummikub?" Dean asked Eliza.

"That sounds perfect," Eliza said, grateful for a distraction.

"If you're lucky, I may even let you win tonight," Dean teased as he pulled the convertible coffee table into its desk mode and retrieved the game from the shelf, setting it on the table.

"Oh, I know you better than that, my love," Eliza winked at Dean and began drawing tiles from the bag, placing them carefully on her tray. "Oh, you're in trouble, Mister," she said, continuing the banter.

As Dean slipped his reading glasses out of the front pocket of his shirt and placed them on his nose, she watched him organize his tiles. She was filled with warm feelings for the first time in more than a few days, and she was reminded again just how lucky she really was.

At that moment, she craved the simple life she once knew, and she decided that she would worry about everything else tomorrow.

Chapter 8

Can you talk?

The text message followed several unread messages from the last few days.

Eliza took a deep breath and answered, *Hi Susan! I can't talk right now because Laura and Dalton are on their way here for the weekend. I'm sorry I've been so out of touch, though. I hope you're doing okay, and I promise I'll call you this weekend after the kids leave.*

She read, and re-read the message a second time, before hitting the blue arrow to send it to her friend. She was relieved when just a second later, Susan replied with a heart emoji.

"Everything okay?" Dean asked, settling down next to Eliza on the other zero gravity lounge chair.

"Oh, yeah," Eliza said. "That was just Susan wanting to chat. I told her that the kids were on their way, which is true, but I'm also just not really wanting to talk to her about everything that happened right now."

Dean looked over, his blue eyes clouded with concern. "How are you feeling?"

"I'm so much better than I was even twenty-four hours ago, but I'm a little nervous about the kids coming and having to talk about everything with them. I just feel kind of fragile, I guess," Eliza said, honestly.

"I'm sure," Dean said. "I'm glad you're feeling better. It's good to have you back out of bed again." He smiled at his wife, and she smiled back.

"I never even asked how *you're* doing," Eliza said, realizing that Dean went through the same thing she did, if not more, since he was actually holding Sharon in his arms when she passed away, and then he immediately had to transition to caretaker for Eliza.

"I'm doing okay," Dean said. "It will be good to have the kids here this weekend. Having the family together is just food for the soul, you know?"

Eliza nodded. "Oh, totally."

They sat together in silence for a few minutes, watching Pupcake explore the yard. "He's checking the perimeter again," Eliza laughed.

Dean chuckled, "Yep, he's a hard worker, keeping us safe and all. I think he's finally starting to get used to wearing that collar."

"Yeah, he's fine with it as long as it's very loose. And he looks good in red," Eliza said, with a giggle.

"I was thinking," Eliza continued after a few moments of silence. "Whatever happened to that middle-aged man that was in the shop when Sharon started choking?"

"A middle-aged man was in the shop? I don't remember that. There was the young couple there, the older lady, and Steve and that other guy, and you, me and Susan. I don't remember anyone else."

"Yeah, there was. He was wearing casual business clothes, like slacks and a collared shirt without a tie. The last I saw him, he was sitting at the table by the door, looking at his phone."

Dean shook his head. "I just don't remember another guy there," he insisted.

"Hm, I'll have to ask Susan what she remembers about him, but he must've left right as the chaos ensued," Eliza thought aloud. "And I need to text George, you know, my delivery guy. Susan said some young kid had delivered the last order and said George was sick. He's never sick. I hope he's okay."

"That is weird. I'm surprised he hasn't reached out to you to ask about deliveries since you're closed temporarily," Dean replied.

"Well, maybe Susan communicated with him. I'll check in with her before I reach out to him."

"Speaking of deliveries, we also never found out who dropped off that package with the sugar, the mugs, and Pupcake's collar. I don't know if anyone will even come out and claim it now," Dean joked.

"Why? Why wouldn't they?" Eliza asked, confused by what he meant.

"I just mean that, you know, Sharon died right after we opened the box."

Eliza sat straight up in her chair. "Dean," she said, grasping the sides of the chair and turning to face her husband. "Do you think..."

"What?" Dean said, "Do I think what?"

Eliza ran her hand through her hair. She lowered her voice. "Do you think Sharon could have been poisoned?"

Dean's eyes clouded with worry again as he tried to make light of the situation. "Well, I certainly hope not, because that wouldn't look good for your coffee."

Eliza gasped. "The bad review, Dean! The bad review said our coffee tasted like poison!"

"Okay, slow down, honey," Dean said. "I'm struggling to keep up with you right now." A ping sound came from his pocket, notifying him of a text. He glanced at it and said, "Well, Laura and Dalton are almost here. Did I tell you that Dalton went and picked up Laura?"

Eliza leaned back in her chair. Worry had taken on a whole new look to Eliza now. Before, she was just worried about the future of the café. Now, she wondered if she had more to worry about than that. She picked up her phone and texted Susan.

Hi again! Weird question. Did you by any chance throw away the empty packaging from the cranberry sugar packet that Sharon added to her coffee the other day?

Eliza hit send and watched her phone for a few seconds, but there was no reply.

"They're here!" Dean said, excitedly jumping up to greet Laura and Dalton. He stopped on his way to the door. "You coming, or you want me to just bring them out here?"

"I'm coming," Eliza said as she rose to her feet and tried desperately to hide her exhaustion and worry and match her husband's enthusiasm. She collected Pupcake from his sunbeam nap and the three of them greeted Laura and Dalton at the door, sharing big long hugs.

"Mom, how are you?" Laura said while squeezing her tight.

"I'm okay, honey," Eliza said, passing Pupcake to her daughter and reaching out to hug Dalton next. "It's so good to have you two home! It feels like Christmas, or something! Come in, come in!" She held the door open as Laura and Pupcake led the way, and the two men followed, carrying their modest luggage.

"Are you all hungry?" Eliza asked, falling right back into Mom mode as if they had never left home.

"Yes! I'm starving!" Dalton said, heading straight for the pantry where the snacks had always been stored. "What's the deal with all this health food?" Dalton laughed. He was about to turn twenty-four, and Eliza thought he looked more and more like his father each year. He was tall and handsome and also had a great head of hair, which he managed to wear thicker and longer while still looking well-groomed. Dalton had hazel eyes like his mother, though, instead of the crystal blue eyes that his father was blessed with, but otherwise, they were starting to look like doppelgängers.

"We can't eat like you guys do anymore," Dean teased his son, ruffling his hair like he used to do when Dalton was only twelve. "You're growing a beard, son?"

Dalton pushed his dad's hand away and rolled his eyes. "Nah, I just didn't shave this morning. My beard grows super fast. It's a pain in the butt."

"Well, you got that honestly," Eliza said. "Your dad has to shave every single day or he will practically have a full grown beard by dinner." They shared a laugh. Dean winked at Eliza, the worry in his eyes replaced by happiness. Pupcake was busy sniffing everyone's shoes, collecting information as to where Laura and Dalton had been all this time. He seemed particularly stuck on Laura's shoes, for some reason.

"We're going to eat dinner soon, Son," Dean said, closing the snack cabinet. "Don't ruin your appetite. I have one of those family size lasagnas from Ferraro's in the oven. It will be ready in an hour or so."

"Yes, let's go sit outside while we wait," Eliza said. "Grab yourselves some sweet tea, if you'd like and meet me out there." Eliza scooped up Pupcake and headed back outside. She sat down in one of the comfortable chairs at the patio table and set Pupcake in the chair next to her. She turned the handle on the umbrella to raise the umbrella, shielding the sun as best she could. Once the umbrella was in position, she sat back down and Pupcake jumped into her lap, plopping down for another nap.

She checked her phone. No new text messages from Susan, or anyone else, for that matter.

The door opened, and Laura led Dalton and Dean outside. A whiff of delicious tomato sauce and mozzarella cheese wafted out of the house.

"Mmmm, that lasagna is going to be delicious," Eliza said.

"Oh my gosh, I'm so excited about it," Laura said. "I have been craving that lasagna for weeks now." She settled in next to Eliza and began petting Pupcake. Dean and Dalton sat in the chairs across the table from them, setting the glasses of iced tea on the table.

"I've missed this little guy, too," Laura said. "Look at his cute collar! I didn't know you were wearing collars now, Fancy Boy," she petted his cheek as he lay in Eliza's lap with his eyes closed.

"Yeah, he got that as a gift," Dean said. He was talking to Laura, but looking at Eliza. "We have no idea who sent it, but it was nice." He shrugged.

"What do you mean?" Dalton asked.

"A package was dropped off at the café the other day with a weird note that read something like, *This is to celebrate your big day*. No one signed it or anything," Eliza said.

"It was dropped off on Monday?" Dalton asked.

"Mmhmm," Eliza said, taking a sip of her tea. "Yeah, the day of the interview." Eliza kept a poker face but her stomach was turning circles. She knew it was going to come up, but she had hoped it wouldn't be right away like this.

"Well, Pupcake must be famous, then," Laura said, "if he's getting anonymous gifts like that." Eliza shot her daughter a look of gratitude. She recognized that she was trying to steer the conversation away from that terrible day.

"He is pretty famous around here," Dean said, "but so is your mom. The package had stuff for her in it, too." He grinned at Eliza.

"Oh?" Dalton said, curious to hear more.

Eliza nodded. "Yes, yes it did. I don't know if I'd say I'm famous, but yes, whoever this special gift giver was, sent some really awesome little flavored sugar packets. I didn't realize that there was such a variety of flavored sugar, but it's a really great idea to offer those to my customers."

"Oh, yeah, that's a great idea," Laura said. "I saw some of those just recently at a local little tea shop in Knoxville."

Eliza took another sip of her tea and checked her phone again. Still no new messages.

"Speaking of Knoxville, how was the drive in?" Dean asked.

"So easy," Dalton said. "No problems at all. I could do without Laura's taste in music, though." He rolled his eyes.

"Oh stop," Laura said. "You were totally singing along to The Lovin' Spoonful!"

"What?!" Dean chimed in. "Those are some great tunes! Real classics." He broke into song, "What a day for a daydream... what a day for a daydreamin' boy..."

Laura chimed in and Dean stood up, grabbing her hand and dancing with her as they sang together. "And I'm lost in a daydream... dreaming 'bout my bundle of joy..."

Dalton tapped the table, keeping the rhythm and picking up the whistling solo when it was time.

"...and you can be sure that if you're feeling right... a daydream will last long into the night..."

Eliza leaned back in her chair, her shoulders finally relaxed. Her and Pupcake sat still and watched, a big smile spread across her face. Pupcake's tail wagged back and forth, his ears perked, taking it all in.

All of Eliza's worries had faded away even if just for a few moments. She was loving every minute of the show and wished that she could stop time for a little while.

Again, she found herself blinking back tears, but this time, they were tears of joy.

Chapter 9

Eliza settled into the easy chair by the large window in the living room. From her vantage point, she could see Pupcake and Dean sitting together outside on the back patio. Dean was lying stretched out in the lounge chair with Pupcake in similar stretched out fashion in Dean's lap. Both appeared to be taking a nap in the sun.

After sending the kids off with yummy leftover lasagna and a few of the lemon tart cupcakes she had brought home from the café, Eliza was happy to take a moment to sit quietly with her thoughts. She needed to make some big decisions on not only how she was going to pick herself up from the terrible event that had happened the week before, but she also needed to decide what she was going to do about the café. She knew that if The Pupcake Café stayed closed too long, it would not be good for business, and the truth was that she missed being there.

She pulled her phone out of her pocket and checked her messages. There was nothing new to look at. Susan had gone quiet, never answering her question about the sugar packaging. She wondered how her friend was doing and knew that she owed her a phone call, but first, she needed to make a list.

For as long as Eliza could remember, making lists and marking things complete had a sort of therapeutic effect. Whenever she felt overwhelmed, she would make a list of her worries, which would soon turn into a list of tasks to complete to overcome them. She lived her life by lists. Her family teased her about her vacation packing lists, followed by her lists of things to do while on vacation. She even had lists reminding her of things she wanted to talk about with Dean over dinner, and of course she had lists of things to do around the house, categorized by season, level of difficulty, and more.

Opening her favorite checklist app on her phone, she began to unravel and unload all the worries in her brain onto her screen.

Decide when to reopen the café, she assigned as the first item on the list.

Decide how to approach the subject of what happened when it comes up, as she typed this task, the familiar pit in her stomach grew and her mind began to race. She shook her head. She knew that everyone was going to want to know what happened, but she also wondered the same thing. She didn't have a clear answer and she needed to find the right way to relay that while remaining respectful to Sharon and to Joe as the chief of police and only one who appeared to be investigating Sharon's death.

She worried that if she explained that Sharon had choked on something and died, it would not be a good look for The Pupcake Café. And even just thinking that way made her feel as if she was heartless and uncaring, and as if she needed to hide something.

Eliza ran her hand through her hair, a nervous habit she had when she was stressed out about something. Her thoughts shifted back to the Yelp review and to the email she received. She wondered if Chief Mason was looking into a correlation between the two. She typed, *Follow up with Chief Mason and ask about the review and email.*

She opened that task and began adding more notes as subtasks. *Tell him about the other customer*, she added, her fingers flying faster over the phone's keyboard as Eliza's worries and thoughts flowed onto the screen. There was something about that other customer she couldn't shake. She had never seen him before, and she didn't see him leave amidst all the chaos of what was happening. For those reasons alone, she thought he might be important to mention.

Talk about the young delivery guy and the wrong order we received. She wasn't sure that was anything to discuss at all, but it was on her mind and she was trying to be thorough.

Talk about the anonymous gift package, Eliza added as another subtask.

Eliza slid the phone back into her pocket, feeling tired all of a sudden. Her head felt cloudy and she desperately needed some answers. She decided to make herself a cup of tea, so she rose to her feet and turned on the electric kettle, watching as the water began to heat up, small bubbles rising slowly to the top. She leaned forward to check on Pupcake and Dean who remained in their exact same poses as before. She noticed how the little stones on Pupcake's collar glowed brightly in the sun. She thought it was so cute how he had finally taken to wearing the collar.

A chime from her phone interrupted Eliza's thoughts and pulling the phone out of her pocket, she saw a message from Laura.

Hi, Mom! I'm back at the dorm, safe and sound. I had a great time this weekend! I hope you have a good week!

Eliza smiled and texted back. *We had fun, too, honey! Just sorry we didn't get to meet Carter!*

Laura responded right away. *He ended up having to leave town this weekend, too, I just found out when I got here. Some family stuff, he said.* She sent the shrugging emoji.

Hmmm, Eliza texted. *I hope everything is okay?*

He seemed totally fine when I texted him this weekend from Copeland. I'm sure it's probably nothing major.

Well, have a good week, too, Laura! Call me soon! Eliza hit send and turned to pour hot water over the Double Bergamot tea bag in her favorite teacup. Her thoughts quickly returned to her list.

Place a new inventory order and add coffee, she typed as a new list item. She wasn't sure when she would reopen but she knew she would need a few things when the time came. Then, she quickly typed, *Check in on George.* She was worried about him after Susan had said that the young delivery guy said George was sick. In the six months since she had opened The Pupcake Café, George was never sick nor did he ever deliver the wrong order.

Setting her phone on the counter, she raised her arms toward the ceiling, arching her back slightly for a nice full stretch. She bent over at the waist into a forward fold yoga pose, focusing on breathing long full breaths for the remaining few minutes her tea needed to steep.

Her phone rang. Eliza raised her head slowly and saw that the caller was Susan. Without hesitation, she answered.

"Hi, Susan," Eliza said, in a friendly tone. "I swear I was about to call you," she laughed.

"Hi! How are you, Ellie?" Susan sounded sincerely concerned for her friend. "I have been so worried, but I know you said that Laura and Dalton were visiting this weekend, so I didn't want to bother you."

"Thanks, Susan," Eliza said. "I'm doing a bit better, and having the kids here played a big part in that. I'm sorry I didn't call you sooner."

"Oh, it's fine," Susan said. "I wasn't sure if they had left yet, but I assumed..."

"Yes, Laura had to get back to prep for an exam tomorrow," Eliza said. "How are you holding up?"

Susan sighed. "Well, I'm okay, too, but I just wish this whole thing had never happened."

Eliza thought, *Me too,* but remained silent.

Susan continued without missing a beat, "I've just been laying low. I don't know what people are saying or thinking, and I don't really want to answer any questions. I honestly don't even know what to say if someone asks me what happened."

"Yeah," Eliza agreed. The one thing about a phone call with Susan is that Eliza could mostly just sit and listen which felt especially nice that day.

"I have been thinking, though," Susan said, "and I keep playing that day over and over in my mind. Sharon was so kind and had such great energy. These things just happen to the best people, you know?" Susan asked the question but didn't give Eliza time to respond before she continued. "I mean to choke on coffee. Who would even think that could happen? I've heard of death by chocolate but not death by coffee. But I guess it's possible to even choke on water, so there's that. Have you heard anything new? Not that I expect to hear anything really. I think Chief Mason got everything he needed that day. He is such a sweet man, and good looking too. I would totally date him now that I'm single. I mean, I could do worse for myself than the chief of police, right? And I think he was kinda giving off vibes that he might be feeling it, too, but can you imagine it? A love story that starts with a murder witness interview? Wouldn't that just be the talk of town, too." She laughed.

Eliza cringed. She knew that Susan meant no harm, but it felt wrong to be so light-hearted about Sharon's murder.

When Susan finally took a breath, Eliza responded. "That would be something else," she said, hoping she didn't sound condescending.

"Oh!" Susan exclaimed before Eliza could continue. "I got your text message. Weird question, but yes, I did throw away the sugar packet in the trash can by the coffee stand. Why? Are you thinking Sharon was poisoned by the sugar or something?" Susan chuckled as if it were preposterous.

"I'm not thinking anything..." Eliza said.

"Oh, I know," Susan interrupted. "But the chief already got the sugar packet out of the trash. You don't remember that? I'm sure they're testing it for something, which is hilarious to me because I can't imagine someone actually being murdered in this town. I mean, on purpose and all."

"The whole day is such a blur to me. I was thinking that I didn't remember anyone collecting evidence, but I guess they did," Eliza said.

"Yeah, they totally did," Susan said. "Now that you say that, I'm reminded of an episode of *To Kill or Not to Kill*. You know that mystery show I watch? It comes on every Wednesday night." Eliza pulled her tea bag out of her cup and dropped it in the compost container on the kitchen counter by the sink. She grabbed her mug and headed back to her comfortable chair. Dean and Pupcake were in the same spot as before.

"Anyway, in the episode I'm thinking about, the killer poisoned someone's food. That's how I knew that some poisons don't have a distinct taste. Remember I said that the other day when we were talking about the Yelp review?"

Eliza sat up straighter in her chair. Something was nagging at her and she couldn't place it. It was like she had a thought just on the brink of forming words.

"So, did they get caught?" Eliza asked.

"Who?" Susan asked. "Did who get caught?"

"The killer in the TV show," Eliza said.

"Oooohhh," Susan said, returning to the conversation. "No, actually. In that episode, the restaurant owner was framed because..." She stopped mid-sentence realizing what she was saying.

Eliza's heart dropped into her stomach. She was silent, but her mind was racing like a hungry greyhound. Susan was saying the one thing that Eliza was trying with all her might to avoid even thinking about.

Not only was it possible that Sharon was murdered, but if it came back that there was indeed foul play that took place in The Pupcake Café that fateful day, she could be looked at as the prime suspect in this whole thing. Susan continued rambling but Eliza didn't hear any of it.

Suddenly, Eliza's doorbell rang.

"I have to go, Susan. Someone is at the door," Eliza said. "I'll call you back later because there's still some things I want to talk to you about."

"Oh, okay. No problem," Susan said. "But, please do call. I want to talk about when we're going to reopen the café."

Eliza promised she would as the doorbell rang a second time. On her feet, Eliza hung up the phone and headed for the door. She looked through the peephole and gasped. There, on the other side of the door, stood Chief Joe Mason, and she could only imagine why he was there.

Chapter 10

Dean sat down across from his wife, mimicking her posture, his back against the arm of the couch. Pupcake was settled in Eliza's lap, his head leaning against her chest listening to her heartbeat.

"Now wait a minute," he said. "Joe didn't say anything about you being a suspect."

"What?" Eliza felt exasperated. "Were we in the same room just now? He totally implied it. Sharon was poisoned, Dean. In my café." Eliza shuddered. Hearing the news that Sharon's autopsy report revealed that the cause of death was cyanide, she felt like she was trapped in a bad movie.

"I think he was trying to intimidate me, hoping I'd confess to something I didn't do."

"So, that's not how I saw things in the conversation we just had, and I feel like you might be overreacting a little bit, honey. You're under a lot of stress. I mean, it makes total sense."

Eliza wiped the tears that streamed down her face with the palms of her hands. "Dean, I'm not going crazy. He wouldn't answer any of my questions, and he kept talking about all the evidence he collected. Why did he even come over here?"

Eliza looked at Dean with pleading eyes. She needed him to tell her everything was going to be alright.

Dean climbed closer to his wife and leaned in wrapping her in a hug. "Honey, it's okay. Joe knows you didn't, or would never, kill Sharon. I mean, even if you were a suspect, what would be your motive? If anyone besides Sharon had a lot to lose here, it would be you. You were supposed to have a big interview and magazine feature, for Pete's sake."

"Well, that's a good point," Eliza mumbled into his shoulder. Dean was probably right. It didn't make sense for the police to suspect her. Her shoulders moved an inch or two away from her ears.

Dean straightened back up, his eyes kind as he held Eliza's shoulders.

"Joe was searching for answers. He was hoping that we would remember something else from that day. Something that would lead him to the answers we all want. I wouldn't want his job right now, I'll tell you that," Dean said.

"I want answers, too," Eliza said meekly. "He didn't know any more about who wrote the review or who sent the email, and I don't know how he could think these things weren't related to what happened. All he is focused on is that stupid package and the cranberry sugar."

"Agreed, but to be fair, the cranberry sugar turned out to be the murder weapon." Dean said. "But you're right. There's definitely something we're all missing. Someone had to have seen who dropped off that package." He took a deep breath before continuing. "However," he paused and held Eliza's gaze as he spoke, "Joe was very clear about you not going around and trying to get involved in the investigation. This is no little crime. There is a murderer out there, and it's not safe for you to go sniffing around trying to get all caught up in it."

Eliza turned and set her feet on the floor, her hand resting on Dean's knee. She heard what Dean was saying, but The Pupcake Café's reputation was at stake. She needed to get to the bottom of it and fast in order to save her business. She turned to Dean and told him what he wanted to hear.

"Of course, honey," she said, rubbing her eyes to avoid eye contact. "I'll leave it to the professionals," she mumbled inside a yawn. She continued acting disinterested, lifting Pupcake up to her lap and scratching him behind the ears. Then, using the oldest distraction trick in the book, she changed the subject.

"Pupcake and I will be headed back to the café today to clean up and place an order for inventory," Eliza said, matter-of-factly. It was true that she needed to do those things, but she had more plans than that for her day. She wanted to contact George and find out about the strange delivery guy and the wrong order, as well as try to track down the customer that mysteriously left right as Sharon began showing symptoms of being poisoned.

It's not that she wanted to lie to Dean, but she worried that he would try to stop her from doing some of her own investigating. She justified it as a half-truth instead and quickly leaned in for a kiss for yet another distraction.

Dean responded by pulling her body closer to his and finishing the kiss with another of his wonderful tight hugs.

"Just promise me you'll be smart and stay out of trouble," he said in a low voice, close to her ear. Pulling back, he gave Pupcake a kiss on the head and rose to his feet, turning to get ready to head out to the office. Over his shoulder he said, "And call me if you need anything at all. I don't have court today. I'm just catching up on work in the office, so I can come running anytime you need me."

Eliza smiled as she stood, holding Pupcake in her arms, and walked Dean to the door. There was no fooling her husband. She was sure he knew exactly what her day's plans were, and Eliza drew a sense of comfort knowing that he would be closely watching for her call if she needed him.

"See you at dinner, honey! I'll cook cheesy pork chops," she called out from the front door as he opened the car door.

"Oh yum! That already sounds amazing," Dean said, standing on one foot, the other propped inside the floorboard. "Pupcake, take care of Mom," Dean said with a grin. Pupcake wagged his tail back and forth as to communicate that he would love nothing more.

Dean climbed into his car and rolled down the passenger window. He leaned over and called out, "I'm serious, Eliza, please be careful today."

Eliza promised she would, and they blew each other kisses before Dean drove out of the driveway and off to work.

"Eliza!" The Campbells' neighbor, Misty Alistair, called out her name from her yard next door. She was holding a water hose over the perfectly pruned landscaping in her front yard, feeding the beautiful purple lilacs and pink tulips that were starting to show growth. She set the hose down and met Eliza halfway to chat.

"How are you? I've been meaning to check on you, but I saw the kids were visiting and didn't want to bother you," Misty said. "I heard what happened, well, it's made big news in Copeland actually. Everyone is talking about it."

Eliza worked hard to keep a smile plastered on her face. She mostly tolerated Misty as a neighbor, especially knowing that Misty had become a widow over ten years ago. Eliza could only imagine how lonely her neighbor must be, and she worked hard to show her compassion.

But, Eliza also knew from experience that Misty was known to be the first to spread gossip around town when she had the opportunity to do so.

"Yes," Eliza nodded. "It was quite terrible." She shifted Pupcake to her right arm.

Misty reached over and petted Pupcake lightly on the head. He leaned forward, stretching his neck out to get even closer.

"So, do they know what happened? People are saying that a woman reporter was poisoned by someone in your little coffee shop. I saw Chief Mason came by your house. You're not in trouble, are you?" The questions came fast and hard, and Eliza shifted from one foot to the other, her stomach tied in knots. She was afraid of what people were saying about the café, and Misty was confirming that her fears were legitimate.

"No, no, nothing like that," Eliza said. "The police did confirm that Sharon was poisoned, but they're still trying to get to the bottom of how it all happened. Of course, no one in my shop actually killed her. Why would we do that?" Eliza asked, leaning in on what Dean was saying just before he left. "No one in my shop would have any reason to kill the editor of the *Sugar and Spice* magazine. That just doesn't make any sense."

Misty nodded, energetically. "Oh, well, of course," she said. "It's just silly rumors circling around. That's all. You know how this town gets." She shrugged her shoulders. "I just can't imagine what you must be going through."

Eliza swallowed the lump in her throat and pushed back the tears she felt forming. She was instantly frustrated at herself for starting to become emotional again when she felt so much stronger just minutes earlier. She stood taller and assured Misty that she was fine.

"Yes, it has been a lot," she confirmed. "But having the kids home for the weekend helped so much."

"Oh good," Misty said. "Everyone is wondering when you're going to reopen your shop, too."

Eliza felt a sense of relief and managed a grin. "Well, Pupcake and I are headed into the café this morning to clean up and assess the situation. Just tell your friends that we'll be open again before you know it."

Relieved that the conversation steered away to the weather and the beautiful flowers, Eliza soon excused herself and headed back inside with Pupcake wiggling in her arms to look back at Misty as they walked away.

Closing the front door behind them, she set Pupcake on the floor and said, "Well, little guy, it looks like we have our work cut out for us to prove these rumors wrong. Let's get ready to go."

Pupcake wagged his tail and turned a circle, following close to her feet as she went about preparing to leave the house for the day.

Piled into the car, the key in the ignition, her phone chimed with a text message. It was from Laura.

Hi Mom! How are you feeling? Can I bring Carter home this weekend? He's back in town and really wants to meet you and Dad.

Chapter 11

E liza unlocked the back door to The Pupcake Café and pushed the heavy door open, Pupcake in one arm, her phone and keys in the other. Dust particles floated in the stale air as if she had been away longer than a week. She missed the smell of the baked goods that would linger from the previous day. She decided she would bake something before she headed home in a couple hours, but first things first. She needed to take inventory and do some general cleaning.

Closing the door behind her and locking it, she set Pupcake down on the floor. He tilted his head, his big shiny eyes looking up at Eliza, and stayed put at her feet.

"What's the matter, Pupcake?" Eliza asked, bending at the knees so that she could be closer to him on the floor. She couldn't tell if his expression was one of fear or just concern, but she realized he must remember the terrible incident that took place just days prior. They'd been home for several days, safe and sound, while Eliza recovered from what happened, but now it was time to get back to work. Eliza knew she had to get her life back on track, and that meant reopening the café.

"It's okay, kiddo," she said, scooping him back up into her arms. "I'm scared, too." She planted a kiss on his tiny head and he leaned into her chest, quiet as a mouse, his tail wagging now that he was back in her arms.

She opened one of the lockers, set her purse and keys inside and pulled out a sling she kept there in case she ever needed to use it. Up until now, it hadn't been necessary. Pupcake had always been very comfortable in what she referred to as their second home. She wondered what and how long it would take for her sweet little pup to get back to that place again. *Well*, she thought, *I should ask myself the same question*. How long would it take *her* to feel normal again, she wondered.

She slipped the sling over her head and Pupcake quickly became situated inside. He was an old hat at finding just the right place to sit in the sling so that he could feel safe up against her chest but still see everything around him. She was always surprised that with Pupcake wrapped up tight in the sling, she was still able to move around and get things done rather efficiently. So, she started about her tasks, beginning with the most dreaded of tasks: assessing the dining area. She knew that they had left the place a mess, hurriedly retreating for their homes as soon as they were given permission from the police to leave. She had mentally prepared to find the mess that they left behind and was anxious to return things to order.

Eliza took a deep breath and approached the front counter, passing a sink full of dirty dishes on the way. The very first thing she noticed were crumbs and circular cup markings on the counter near the cash register and over the empty pastry case. The tables and chairs in the dining area looked mostly clean, but Eliza knew they needed to be wiped down, too.

At the coffee station, trash from little creamer cups and sugar packets were scattered around. Eliza's stomach dropped when she spotted the remaining unopened flavored sugar packets she had received as a gift displayed neatly on a platter. A flash of memories took over as she remembered being so excited to open the box and find what she thought were cute little sugar packets. Now, she only saw skulls and crossbones, wondering if any other flavors were also poisonous.

She rushed over to the station and dumped the platter's contents into the garbage along with the creamer packaging. Standing close enough, she unwillingly got a whiff of the trash in the trash bag and instantly regretted not taking that out before they left that evening, but taking the trash out and cleaning up were the absolute last things on anyone's mind that fateful evening.

She pulled the full trash bag out of the can and tied it tight, carrying it to the back and setting it by the back door. No doubt, there would be more trash to collect before she was done.

Returning to the dining area, her eyes were next drawn to Pupcake's little area where she saw what she dreaded seeing the most, pieces of Sharon's broken cup and what remained of her coffee, spread out and now dried to the black and white floor tiles.

"Oh my goodness," she said aloud, remembering how Chief Mason was adamant that she not clean up the mess right away due to evidence collection.

She bent down to pick up the pieces of the shattered ceramic mug, stacking them in her hand. Another memory flashed through her mind, and she could picture just how excited Sharon was to taste her coffee. Eliza could remember how proud she felt in that moment to have someone like Sharon tell her how delicious her coffee was, especially after the bad review the café had received. If only she had known, or had even questioned the flavored sugar, maybe the outcome would have been very different.

Returning to the kitchen, she dumped the ceramic pieces into the trash and looked around. Aside from the dirty dishes, the kitchen was tidy for the most part. Only a few measuring cups and spoons were left out. All food was put away, much to Eliza's relief.

Eliza returned to the back door area and slipped a clean apron over her head and under Pupcake's sling, the motion waking him from what appeared to be another light nap. She pulled on some rubber gloves and dove into cleaning, starting with all of the surfaces, Pupcake in tow. After all the surfaces were cleaned, she tackled the floors, mopping them until they shone like new again. All that remained was to wash the dishes. She decided to take a break as the floors dried and settled in with a glass of iced water and a protein bar she had found in the bottom of her purse. Pupcake watched every bite as it moved from her hand to her mouth.

"I'm sorry, baby," Eliza said, "You can't have any of this." She removed Pupcake from the sling and tiptoed out the front door to give him a potty break on the narrow strip of grass between the sidewalk and the street in front of the café. Waiting for him to finish, Eliza glanced around at the activity on the quiet street. She felt invisible, and she didn't mind that at all at this moment.

Scooping Pupcake back up into her arms, she headed inside and locked the door behind her. The floors had dried enough to set him down, and she watched as he proceeded to sniff the perimeter of the room. He kept glancing back at Eliza as if to keep her in eyesight, still a little wary of not sticking right by her side, so she settled into a chair at one of the dining tables and pulled out her phone. She glanced at her task list.

Check in on George, she read. She searched the contacts, found his number, and placed the call. It rang a few times before George's familiar voice answered, the sound of traffic in the background.

"Hello?" He answered.

"Hi, George! It's Eliza Campbell from The Pupcake Café. How are you?"

"Oh, hi, Mrs. Campbell! I'm fine, but I think I should be asking you how you're doing?"

"Well, you know..." Eliza found herself stuttering. For some reason, she wasn't expecting that question and wasn't sure how to answer it. "I'll be okay. Thank you for asking, George."

"I was so sorry to hear about what happened, Mrs. Campbell," George continued. "I think we're all shocked that something like that took place in our little town."

"Yeah, well, I know," Eliza said. "Me too."

"Please let me know if there's anything I can do for you ladies," George said.

"Thanks again, George. I was actually calling because I think we had the wrong order delivered last week. It was a different delivery guy, and he said you were out sick. I wanted to check in on you." She braced herself for George's answer.

"Oh, right. That was Marty. He was covering for me. I had tested positive for that stupid coronavirus, and I was out for that whole week."

Eliza slowly released the breath she didn't realize she was holding.

George continued, "I'm sorry about the wrong order, though. If it's any consolation, you weren't the only one who got the wrong stuff. Someone else probably got yours. I can deliver whatever you need, though, just let me know."

"No worries at all, George. I'm sorry to hear you were sick, but it sounds like you're feeling better and back to work?"

"Yes, I'm feeling much better, thank you, ma'am, and I've tested negative a few times now so I'm safe to get back out into the world again," he chuckled.

"That is good to hear, George," Eliza said. "I'll place an order this afternoon, but there's no rush. I'm closed temporarily right now and still on the fence about when

I'm reopening. I'll make a decision and add a delivery date in the details of the order, if that's okay with you."

"Yes, totally fine," George said. "And I'll make sure you get your money back on that wrong order, too."

"That sounds fine," Eliza said. "Thank you, and take care of yourself."

"I'll see you soon, Mrs. Campbell. Hang in there, and have a good day!"

Eliza thanked him again and ended the call. She took a deep breath and exhaled slowly. So, there was no mystery there. George had just been sick.

She marked that task complete and moved on. The next task was to take inventory, but she skipped ahead to the task that reminded her she was going to try and find out who the other customer was that had coincidentally disappeared when Sharon was fighting for her life.

She rifled through the receipts from that last day, considering the timing. If she remembered correctly, he would have been the third to last party that was checked out that day. Mrs. Wilson was the very last and the three young women were just before her. The mystery man was alone and the couple was right before him. Studying the tickets closely, Eliza was able to decipher exactly which ticket was his, and unfortunately, he had paid in cash. The only name on the ticket was Jeff. That wasn't going to answer any questions for her at all. It was another dead end.

Eliza was a bit disappointed and quite frustrated to come up empty handed, but she had always told her kids that when you're trying to find an answer, the process of elimination can be very valuable in the search. So, she resigned to be grateful for being able to eliminate the substitute delivery driver and the strange man who shall remain unnamed on her very amateur list of suspects.

Looking over towards the window, she was relieved to see Pupcake settled in his bed. It seemed to represent a touch of normalcy that she was craving. Now, she just needed to tackle those dishes and take inventory. Then, she and Pupcake could head home and start cooking dinner.

As Eliza turned away from the front counter to head towards the kitchen, a knock at the door sent her heart racing. She turned to see Mrs. Wilson standing on the other side of the locked glass door, waving and smiling.

"Eliza! Hi! Are you open?" Mrs. Wilson asked, excitedly.

Pupcake matched her energy with a couple short barks, running to the door to greet one of his favorite people. Eliza had no choice but to open the door, so she approached with what she hoped wouldn't be recognized as the forced smile that it was. She unlocked the door and pulled it open, inviting Mrs. Wilson inside. Pupcake stood on his back legs, his front paws bouncing off Mrs. Wilson's ankles.

"Hi, Mrs. Wilson," Eliza said. "It's good to see you, but I'm actually only here cleaning."

"Oh, my gosh, I'm sorry to bother you, then," Mrs. Wilson said. "I just saw you in here and *had* to say hello. When are you going to reopen?" Mrs. Wilson bent down to scratch Pupcake behind the ears, as she did each time she visited the café. He was putty in her hands and turned over to get a belly rub.

"I'm not sure just yet," Eliza answered. "I still have some things to do before it's ready," Eliza hated telling untruths to one of her best customers, but she justified it in her mind that it wasn't a total lie. There was inventory to be ordered, and she personally still had a lot of healing to do.

"Well, how are you holding up?" Mrs. Wilson asked.

"I'm doing well," Eliza answered. "How are you? I can't apologize enough for what happened here the other night." Eliza hung her head and Mrs. Wilson gently squeezed her arm.

"Oh, girlie, it's not your fault at all," Mrs. Wilson said, sympathetically. "I'm okay. I've lived a long life and have seen a lot of things. It takes more than something like that to shake me to my core."

Eliza nodded. "Oh, I'm so glad you're not traumatized by the whole thing. It was just so crazy. I almost still feel like I'm not sure all of that really happened. Like it was some really bad dream or something." She blinked back tears and silently prayed that she wouldn't start crying again. Not in front of Mrs. Wilson.

"Life throws curveballs sometimes," Mrs. Wilson said. "It's all about how you are able to get back up and pick up the pieces, take it from me."

"Yes, those are wise words, indeed," Eliza smiled gratefully.

"Well, I'll let you get back to it so you can finish and get home to that wonderful husband of yours."

"Thank you, Mrs. Wilson. I'll text you when I decide what day I'll reopen," Eliza promised.

"Yes, please do," Mrs. Wilson said, her hand on the door handle. "Before I forget, are you going to attend Ms. McArthur's funeral? You know she was from Smallville, right? Have you been there before?"

Eliza was ready for the conversation to come to an end. She didn't want to talk about Sharon, the incident, or her funeral. "Mmmm," Eliza responded quietly. "I don't think we'll be making it. Are you going?" Eliza asked only to be polite.

"Oh me? No. I didn't even know her that well. I don't know anyone in Copeland who did know her except for Mr. Stewart of course. I'm sure he's probably going to attend the funeral." Mrs. Wilson said, matter-of-factly, taking another step out of the doorway.

Mr. Stewart knew Sharon? Eliza thought to herself, trying to hide the surprise on her face.

"Right. Well, that makes total sense then," Eliza said, not sure what else to say.

The two of them exchanged goodbyes, and Eliza locked the door.

Mr. Stewart knew Sharon? She repeated in her thoughts. She wasn't sure why that was surprising, but she couldn't stop thinking about how she almost ran into him right after the anonymous package was delivered.

Chapter 12

Eliza laid back on the couch, stretching her feet to the other side. Pupcake jumped up onto her legs and settled in, facing her. He blinked his eyes slowly a few times as she watched him, her own eyes feeling tired and heavy from the lack of restless sleep over the past week. Just as she started to doze off, her phone chimed.

She ignored it and continued to relax, uninterrupted.

"Mom?" Eliza woke to Laura's voice, streaming in from the front door. "Mom! We're here!" Her voice rang out traced with a hint of concern.

Pupcake barked, jumped off the couch and ran to greet his sister.

"Oh, well, hi there, Sweetpea," Laura said just before Pupcake erupted into a much less friendly bark mixed with a few growls. "Okay, okay, take it easy," Eliza heard Laura say. "This is Carter, Pupcake, he's our friend."

Eliza was then fully awake, she stood, straightened her shirt and ran her hand through her hair. She wiped under her eyes and took a deep breath. Pupcake continued with what they called his angry bark.

Laura emerged around the corner, Pupcake wiggling in her arms, followed by a young man who looked at least a couple years older than her. Immediately, Eliza thought he looked like Buddy Holly, lanky, with a thin nose and large black-rimmed glasses. Eliza took Pupcake from Laura and held him tight, stroking his fur on his back, trying to calm him down.

"Hi!" Eliza said. "You must be Carter!" She greeted him with a smile, willing to give anyone that Laura was interested in, a fair chance.

"Yes, ma'am," Carter said. "The one and only." He grinned and showed off a beautiful smile with straight white teeth. "Carter Banks," he said, as he extended his hand for a handshake.

"You can call me Eliza," she replied with a nod.

Eliza shook his hand, and Pupcake began throwing another fit, almost jumping out of her arms. "Pupcake, settle down," Eliza said in a more stern voice. Then, she turned to Laura, apologetic, and said, "I guess y'all interrupted his nap." She chuckled.

"Oh, I know what that's like," Carter said. "I am the same way, buddy." He reached out the back of his hand to allow Pupcake to sniff him, and turned his eyes away. Eliza noted that he clearly had experience being around dogs to know this simple trick, and she gave him a point for a good first impression. At first, Pupcake reluctantly sniffed Carter's hand and then gave in to temptation, inching closer to continue his investigation into this new person who just walked into his house.

"Sorry we interrupted your nap, Mom," Laura said, leaning in for a hug interrupting Pupcake's introduction to Carter. "I texted when we were close."

"Oh, it's totally fine," Eliza said with a smile. "That couch gets me everytime," she said with a wink. "Come on in! It looks nice outside, would you like to go sit out on the patio?"

Laura looked at Carter for approval and they answered, "Sure" in unison, followed by laughter. Carter put his arm around Laura and pulled her closer next to his side. Eliza thought they looked cute together with similar fair skin and dark features.

"Can I get you something to drink?" Eliza asked, heading toward the kitchen. She placed Pupcake down on the floor, watching him closely to make sure he was acting right towards their new guest. He sniffed Carter's shoes as if they told fascinating stories from lands far away, following him around and switching from foot to foot.

"Oh, yes, please. Carter, you're gonna love my mom's sweet tea," Laura said.

"I can't wait," Carter said. "It reminds me of home. We used to always have a pitcher of sweet tea in the fridge when I was growing up."

"Oh yeah?" Eliza asked. "Laura said you grew up in..."

"Louisiana," Carter interrupted. "I grew up in a town called Monroe. It's really close to Mississippi."

"Hmm.. I think I may have heard of it," she said.

"There's not much there," Carter said. "Except my parents," he winked and flashed another bright smile.

"When's Dad coming home, Mom?" Laura said, as they settled into the patio chairs at the outside table.

"He won't be home until dinner, I'm afraid," Eliza said. "He has a lot of work he has to catch up on since..." She let her words trail off, instantly regretting bringing up the prior week's incident that required Dean to take a lot of time off from his business. Quickly changing the subject, she explained to Carter, "He's a personal injury attorney."

"Yes, that's what Laura tells me," Carter said. "That's fascinating work."

Eliza sensed a bit of sarcasm, but she couldn't be sure.

Laura reached down and scooped up Pupcake. She let him lick her face before she planted a few kisses on his cheeks.

"How is school going, Carter?" Eliza asked. "Laura tells us you're studying Communications?"

"That's right," Carter said, seemingly distracted by watching Pupcake play with Laura.

A gentle breeze swept by, and Eliza closed her eyes, enjoying the perfect seventies temperature.

"Do you want to sit with Carter?" Laura was asking Pupcake. Eliza opened her eyes and watched as Pupcake reluctantly sat with this new person. He never took his eyes off of Eliza's face.

"Good boy," Eliza said, smiling. "See? He can have good manners, I swear," she laughed.

After taking another sip of tea, Eliza asked Laura and Carter, "So, is there anything you want to do today?"

Laura answered for the both of them, "Well, Carter really wants to see The Pupcake Café."

Ugh, Eliza thought to herself, still feeling tired from an unfinished nap. She didn't feel up to showing guests around town, but she also didn't want to be rude.

"Let's do it," she said instead, with forced enthusiasm that she hoped was mistaken for the real thing.

"If you're sure," Laura said, probably picking up on her mother's energy.

"Of course I'm sure!" Eliza said, convincingly. "I'm just going to freshen up real quick, and then we'll head out. We can easily be back in time to throw dinner on for when your dad gets home." She got up and headed inside. Pupcake jumped out of Carter's lap and followed Eliza into the house.

A few minutes later, the four of them were on their way to the café, chatting mostly about the classes Laura and Carter were taking. Eliza couldn't help but notice that Carter was recording a lot of video on his phone. Some of the coverage seemed to include the view of the town from the backseat, but most of the videos seemed to be front facing, with himself centered on the screen. It sure seemed to Eliza that Carter knew a lot about Copeland as he described the parks and shops they passed. She imagined he must have done quite a bit of research before coming to visit.

Since they were just going to be in and out of the café, Eliza decided to park on the street. She avoided Carter's camera as much as possible as she approached the front door and unlocked it.

"Oh wow, this place is great!" Carter said, looking at the cafe through the screen of his phone. Laura switched places from his side to behind him, depending on the vantage point, as if she had been exposed to Carter's documentary creation on several occasions and knew just what to do to also avoid the camera.

Carter swung the camera around to capture Eliza. "There she is, ladies and gentlemen," Carter said in a performative voice, "The brains behind The Pupcake Café, meet the owner, Mrs. Eliza Campbell. And of course, we can't forget the coffee shop's namesake, Mr. Pupcake!" He zoomed in on Pupcake's face and then zoomed back out again.

Eliza fidgeted, holding Pupcake closer to her, and smiled awkwardly, her eyes fixed on Carter, not the phone thrust in front of her. Laura insisted on showing Carter around, escorting him but staying off camera as he recorded everything. Eliza wasn't sure how she felt about all of The Pupcake Café being captured on camera, but she didn't have anything to hide, and she assumed the video wouldn't go viral or anything like that, if he were to publish it..

The young couple came around the corner, their tour complete, and the four of them headed back outside. The camera was still rolling as Carter continued to narrate everything he saw. Eliza turned to lock the door behind them when she heard a familiar voice speaking behind her.

"Peter?" Eliza turned to find Mr. Stewart speaking to Carter. Clearly, he was confused as to who he was speaking to.

Eliza thought Carter looked uncomfortable. He didn't answer. He stopped recording and tried to open the locked car door.

"Peter," Mr. Stewart repeated. "You probably don't remember me," he said. "The last time I saw you, you were much younger."

There was still an awkward silence. Finally, Carter responded, "I think you've got the wrong guy, sir." Then, he turned to Laura and said impatiently, "Are we ready?"

Laura nodded, and Eliza clicked the remote to unlock the car. Carter slipped inside quickly and shut the door. Laura climbed into the front seat. Eliza watched as Mr. Stewart shook his head and continued on his way. Feeling as if they might have all been rude, Eliza called out, "Have a good day, Mr. Stewart!"

The conversation was a bit different on the ride back to the house.

"I wonder what that was about," Laura said.

"That old man clearly had dementia or something," Carter quickly answered. "As a matter of fact, there was something just straight creepy about him. Did either of you feel that?"

"Oh, no," Eliza corrected him. "Mr. Stewart is harmless. He's just an old man. I think he has lived in Copeland longer than anyone else. That's what I heard," she said, turning on her blinker and coming to a stop at a stoplight.

"I'm with Carter, Mom," Laura said. "Something just felt weird with all that."

"Yeah," Carter repeated. "He's creepy. No doubt. That guy was confused, with a capital C."

Eliza didn't care for Carter's comments. To her, it felt disrespectful and rude. So what if the old man, Mr. Stewart, thought he was someone else? That didn't necessarily make him creepy. But, she decided to let it go and change the subject.

"Are you all staying the night? I didn't see any luggage," Eliza asked Laura who was looking out the window and mindlessly rubbing Pupcake's tiny ear with her index finger and thumb.

"No," Laura said. "Sorry if I wasn't clear about that, but Carter has to get back for something tomorrow."

"Yeah," Carter chimed in. "I have a big project due on Monday."

Eliza pulled into the driveway. She was actually relieved to hear that they would be leaving after dinner. She absolutely loved it when Laura came to visit, but she wasn't sure she had the energy to host someone else, too.

"Oh, I understand," Eliza said. "At least you're only a couple hours away. That is so nice." She turned off the car and led the way inside, Pupcake still hanging out with Laura.

"Make yourselves at home," Eliza said. "I need to get dinner started." She headed into the kitchen to start peeling potatoes. Laura set Pupcake outside and offered to help.

Carter began recording video again, talking endlessly about what felt to Eliza like nothing at all into the phone.

"Does he do this all the time?" Eliza whispered to Laura as they worked side by side prepping vegetables for a salad.

Laura nodded and giggled. "You get used to it," she said.

"I don't know about that," Eliza said, only half-joking. She peeked through the window to see Pupcake frolicking about, chasing a butterfly.

"He's so cute," Eliza said. "Look at him, Laura. He's chasing a monarch butterfly."

Laura leaned in and agreed that Pupcake was indeed super cute before turning back to the vegetables. "What can I do next?" She asked.

"Um," Eliza paused for a moment before answering. "I would love it if you could grate some cheddar cheese."

"I can do that," Laura said, opening the refrigerator and pulling out the cheese.

"Can you also please grab the pork chops?" Eliza asked politely. "I'll trim those next."

Her attention shifted suddenly when she heard Pupcake scream out in trouble. Her heart felt like it jumped out of her chest and she exchanged a quick glance of panic with Laura before running for the door. The screams were terrible, short, shrill yells for help. He wasn't angry barking. He was in trouble. She threw the door open to find Carter bent over near Pupcake. Eliza wasn't sure what was happening. It didn't look like Carter was even touching him, but she couldn't be sure. She instinctively called Pupcake's name. Pupcake turned his head swiftly toward Eliza and bolted her way, jumping into her open arms as she knelt on the ground.

"What's going on?" Eliza asked Carter, petting Pupcake as he trembled in her arms.

"I don't know," Carter said. "He just started screaming, so I was trying to help him."

Laura stepped outside. "Everybody okay?" She asked.

Carter shrugged, his hands in his pockets. "I hope so," he said. "Whatever it was, it scared the little guy."

Eliza inspected Pupcake for anything strange. "He's okay," she said. "He's just scared. So weird."

She led everyone back inside, Pupcake in her arms. She held the door open for Laura, then Carter. As Carter approached, he pulled his hand out of his pocket to hold the door.

Pupcake's red collar with shiny colored stones fell to the floor just inside the door. Eliza looked at Carter, confused, and Carter looked at Eliza with a look that Eliza could only explain later to Dean as guilty or panicked.

Did Carter try to steal Pupcake's collar? Eliza thought to herself. *Why in the world would he do that?*

Eliza bent down to pick it up off the floor. "Why is your collar off?" She posed the question to Pupcake but she was looking straight at Carter when she asked it.

"That's weird," Carter responded, shrugging it off. He excused himself to the bathroom.

Before Eliza could say anything to Laura about what she just saw, Dean walked in the door and swept her up in a giant bear hug.

The night continued on without missing a beat, except Eliza kept a very close eye on Carter and Pupcake chose to stay in her lap where he felt safe and sound. Dean seemed to enjoy Carter's stories about his childhood growing up as an only child, spoiled rotten by his surgeon father and wonderful mother. Eliza noticed on a few different occasions how happy Laura looked as she held hands with her new boyfriend under the table.

After dinner, they exchanged their goodbyes, and Eliza and Dean wished the young couple a safe drive back to the university.

Relieved that the visit was over, Eliza plopped down on the couch. Pupcake jumped up next to her. He stood on his back legs in her lap and placed his front paws on either side of her neck, leaning in for a hug.

"What a sweet boy I have," Eliza said to Pupcake, stroking his cheek. Pupcake moved off of Eliza's lap and began to scratch his collar, his eyes looking up at his favorite person.

"Why are you scratching, Silly?" Eliza asked, "Did I put it back on too tight? Here, let me take it off."

She pushed the leather strap through the buckle to take it off when something caught her eye. She pulled it off and looked at it more closely. *That's really strange*, she thought to herself. It looked like maybe one of the shiny stones was coming loose.

Dean walked into the room with his glasses and sat down on his end of the couch. "Whatcha lookin at?" He asked.

"It looks like one of the stones is falling out of Pupcake's collar," she said, holding it out to him. Dean took it from her and set his reading glasses on his nose.

"And oh my gosh, I have to tell you what happened tonight with Pupcake and Carter," Eliza said, sitting back and pulling Pupcake close.

Dean inspected the collar closely. Before Eliza could even continue, he said, "This isn't a loose stone, Eliza." He lowered it to his lap and looked at his wife in disbelief. "It's a tiny little spy camera."

Eliza gasped, her hand covered her mouth.

Chapter 13

Eliza approached the front of the police station and pushed the door open. She had to leave Pupcake at home and already missed having him with her.

"Can I help you, Miss?" The uniformed man behind the counter asks.

"Hi, is Chief Mason available?" Eliza asks, fidgeting with the loose thread on the belt loop of her jeans that she somehow only discovered just minutes before.

The man nodded. "Hang tight, I'll grab him," and he disappeared behind a heavy door with a frosted glass window.

Chief Joe Mason emerged from behind the door and greeted Eliza with a smile. Eliza was put at ease when she saw him. She always thought Chief Mason was a nice enough looking guy. His salt and pepper mustache and beard were neatly trimmed and his hair was cut short, most likely to hide the fact that it was thinning. He was an average height for a man, Eliza thought, not too tall or too short with broad shoulders and a fit figure. It was only their interaction at the café the day the incident happened, that Eliza ever felt uncomfortable around the chief, and standing in front of him today, she understood the difference.

"Hi, Eliza! What brings you in here this fine morning?" the chief asked cheerfully.

"Hi, Chief," Eliza said, pulling the dog collar out of her purse. "I have something to show you."

Chief Mason invited Eliza to join him in his office and he escorted her through a door on her right to a small space barely fitting the oversized mahogany desk and two uncomfortable wooden chairs. The desk was tidy and neat, which Eliza found surprising for no other reason than the stereotypical Chief of Police in the mystery TV shows that she watched were always quite the opposite. Their desks would be piled high with papers, old fast food wrappers and such.

"Okay, whatcha got?" Chief Mason asked her, gesturing for her to grab a chair as he settled in his seat across the desk.

Eliza held the collar out for him to see. She placed it on the desk in front of him, explaining that this was included in the anonymous gift package and how they found what they think is a hidden camera.

The chief opened his top desk drawer and pulled out a magnifying glass, inspecting the stones carefully.

"Well, I'll be damned," the chief said. "It does look like a camera." He set it down in front of him and leaned back in his chair, his fingers interlocked together in front of him, resting on his stomach.

"That is really strange," he said, still staring at the collar. "You say this came in the gift package with the sugar packets?"

"Yes," Eliza nodded. "Pupcake has been wearing it the whole time."

She wanted to also mention that she thought she caught her daughter's new boyfriend trying to steal it, but she wasn't completely positive that's what she saw. She figured it was best to keep that to herself until she could actually prove it or at least have more of a convincing reason to accuse him of something like that.

"How did you find it?" Chief Mason asked, again picking it up and inspecting it closer.

Eliza shrugged. "Pupcake started scratching around it last night - he doesn't normally wear collars, you see - so I went to loosen it and decided to just take it off for the night. That's when I thought there was just a loose stone on it. I passed it to Dean to see what he thought it was. And he is the one who figured out what it really is."

"Hmmm... okay, well, I'll send it into forensics and see if they can find out more about it," the chief said. Then looking up, he asked, "Are you doing okay, though?"

Eliza nodded with more confidence than she felt. "Yeah, I'm okay," she answered. "I would feel better if we actually knew who poisoned Sharon, but I'm trying to be patient."

"I know," the chief said sympathetically. "The waiting is the hardest part. Every. Single. Time," he paused between each word. "But, don't lose faith. We'll get them." He smiled a reassuring smile.

"Thank you, Chief," Eliza said. "I appreciate your hard work on this."

"Of course," the chief said, standing to his feet and opening the office door wider. "Thank you for coming in. Tell Dean I said hi."

Eliza stood to leave, assuring him she would pass along the word to her husband. She headed out of the station feeling as if she had accomplished something, but she was ready to go pick up her little buddy. There was one more stop she had in mind for that morning.

After collecting Pupcake, she set the GPS on her phone to take her to 102 Maple Street. Pulling into the tree lined driveway, she could feel butterflies flying around in her stomach. Even Pupcake seemed to fidget quite a bit in his carseat. She stepped out of the car and grabbed Pupcake, slipping him into the sling she had brought with her for convenience. The extra wide porch steps had a slanted ramp fashioned on top of half of them, but she took the steps instead. Standing in front of the door, she saw the name Stewart engraved on the heavy brass door knocker. She lifted the knocker and let it drop twice, and waited patiently.

She could hear shuffling from the other side of the door, faint at first but getting louder as the footsteps moved closer. The sound of unlocking deadbolts could be heard, one after another after another, before the heavy door creaked open. Standing in front of her was old man Mr. Stewart, holding onto a cane for balance. Eliza found herself trying to remember if he was using a cane the last couple times she ran into him and didn't think he was.

"Hi, Mr. Stewart," Eliza said politely. "I don't know if you remember me, but I'm..."

"Eliza Campbell," Mr. Stewart said. "You own that coffee shop with that little dog." He nodded toward Pupcake who sat quiet and still in the sling up against Eliza.

"That's right," Eliza said, not able to hide her surprise.

"What can I do for you, Mrs. Campbell?" Mr. Stewart asked with a flat tone, looking over the wire glasses that sat below the bridge of his nose.

"I, um,..." Eliza stammered. She realized she hadn't been prepared for this obvious direct question. She took a breath before continuing, "I actually hoped I could ask you some questions, if you had a minute and didn't mind?" She felt like her heart was beating out of her chest as she waited for what felt like an eternity for his answer.

"Very well," Mr. Stewart said. "But, if it's all the same to you, I'd like to stay outside and sit down on the porch."

Eliza would never admit that she secretly wanted to see what was inside the old man's house, so she whole-heartedly agreed to sit on the porch with him instead of sitting inside. He gestured toward a couple wicker chairs and she chose one with a blue cushion with yellow flowers. He sat a few seats away on an orange cushion with stripes.

"Thank you for your time, Mr. Stewart," Eliza began. "This won't take long. I just wanted to ask how you knew Sharon McArthur... you know, the lady who died in my café?"

Mr. Stewart leaned back in his chair and said, "Ah, yes. Well, I didn't know Sharon as well as I know her parents. They're good people, as we used to say. My wife, God bless her soul, grew up in Smallville and we went to the McArthur's restaurant every year on her birthday until it mysteriously burned down one day."

"Oh?" Eliza asked, leaning slightly forward with interest.

"Yes," Mr. Stewart said, his eyes fixed on Eliza's and Eliza suddenly had a feeling there was more to the story than that.

"What was the name of the restaurant?" She asked out of curiosity, but also hoping to pull more information out of him.

Mr. Stewart responded slowly, never shifting his eyes and hardly blinking at all. "It was named Juniper, after the gorgeous trees that surrounded it," he answered, waiting for Eliza to respond.

Eliza squinted her eyes trying to remember where she heard the word Juniper recently. She petted Pupcake's neck as he shifted in the sling, searching for a more comfortable position.

Mr. Stewart sat straighter in his chair before speaking again. "I sent you that email," he said pointedly.

Eliza's mouth fell open. That's where she had heard it! It was the sender's email address: Juniper1972@gmail.com.

"But,..." Eliza started to ask the next question when Mr. Stewart cut her off in mid-sentence.

"It was my wife's email address. I saw the review and tried to warn you," the old man said.

"Warn me? Did you know that Sharon was going to be poisoned that day?" Eliza asked the obvious next question.

"Like I said, I've known the McArthur's for many years, and I sensed something fishy was going to happen when I saw that review. You have the most beloved coffee shop that Copeland has ever had, with stellar reviews. When a bad review came up, it didn't take a professional sleuth to see that something weird was going to go down."

Eliza was both flattered and shocked. She sat there quietly as Mr. Stewart continued.

"I like reading reviews," he explained. "It's kind of a hobby of mine." He shrugged. Then, hanging his head, he said, "I just wish I had known that they were going to kill Sharon, so I could've stopped them. She seemed like such a nice girl."

"Yes, I agree," Eliza was able to mumble. "She seemed very nice."

"But, I was really confused when I saw Peter with you and your daughter the other day," Mr. Stewart continued.

"Oh, yeah, my apologies if we were rude that day. You were a bit confused, I'm afraid. That was my daughter's new boyfriend. His name is Carter Banks, not Peter."

Again, with his eyes locked on Eliza's, Mr. Stewart responded. "No, I'm sorry, but you're mistaken." He spoke slowly and deliberately. "That boy looks like a carbon copy of his father. I may be old, but I have no doubt in my mind that the boy that was with you the other day was Peter McArthur."

Eliza's eyes grew big. Could it be? She thought to herself, suddenly remembering the video recordings in the café, the incident with Pupcake's collar, and all the stories he told about his childhood. None of it made sense, yet all of it was starting to make perfect sense as she placed together puzzle piece after puzzle piece in her mind.

Mr. Stewart continued, "Peter is Sharon's younger brother, and I believe you could characterize his relationship with his parents as estranged. That's all I know, though. Family secrets run deep, you know."

Eliza's world had just been rocked. She thanked Mr. Stewart for his time and hurried back to her car. She needed to call Dean and tell him everything. And what about Laura? Was she safe? Eliza couldn't be sure.

Dean was just as shocked as she was when he heard the news. He told her he would meet her at home, to go straight there and lock the doors. He said he would be there just as soon as he could, that he was calling Joe on the way.

Eliza parked the car in the driveway, looking all around before stepping out. She was a nervous wreck. It was peculiar how she was more nervous now that she was pretty sure she knew who the killer was, compared to when she didn't have a name or a face to assign to it. She collected Pupcake and shuffled into the house quickly, locking the doors behind her. She and Pupcake collapsed on the couch, laying there, reliving the conversation she had just had with Mr. Stewart.

Should she believe the old man? How could she know if he was telling the truth? On the one hand, it did seem very believable but on the other, it was almost too much of a coincidence.

How could her daughter's new boyfriend be related to something that happened in her café two hours away... unless that was his whole plan. Maybe that was part of his alibi.

Eliza was feeling overwhelmed and she wished she could just stop thinking about all of it.

The copy of the Sugar and Spice magazine that Steve had passed on from Sharon to Eliza that fateful day was sitting on the coffee table in front of her. She had only just started looking through it earlier that morning, her coffee in hand. Eliza reached out and picked it up to see if there was a bio about Sharon anywhere. As she lifted it off the table, a piece of paper fell to the floor. Eliza leaned down to pick it up and gasped.

It was a note, written in the same red ink with the same child-like handwriting that was on the anonymous gift package. The note read, *Dear Sis - if you know what's good for you, you won't tell them.*

It was signed with the initials PM.

Chapter 14

D alton handed Laura another tissue. He sat on one side of her on the couch, his arm around her, while Eliza sat on the other side, holding her hand. Dean was in the large comfy chair at the end of the couch, leaning forward, his elbows on his knees. Pupcake was in Laura's lap, curled up and pressed up against her as close as he could be.

"This is all so crazy," Laura said between sobs. "I feel so stupid." She had just arrived from the university where Dalton had picked her up and brought her home. Carter, a.k.a. Peter McArthur, had been arrested for his sister's murder, and her world was crashing down around her.

"He fooled all of us, honey," Eliza said. "You're not stupid."

Dean stood and paced back and forth in front of them, running his hand through his hair. "I'm still trying to make sense of all of this. I mean, what was the guy's motive?" Dean asked, frustration clear in his voice.

"Apparently, there was a sibling rivalry between those two for years over who was the favorite. Carter, or Peter, I guess, knew that Sharon was coming into town here for Mom's interview. She had texted him to tell him that she was going to visit their parents and that she was tired of keeping his big secret from them," Laura responded.

"Wait, what was the big secret?" Dalton asked. "Do we know?"

Laura shook her head.

"I think he set the family restaurant on fire and it burned to the ground," Eliza said. "Mr. Stewart had said something about a family secret. I did some research and read about the fire. It was determined that it was an accident, but caused by a town drifter. The poor guy even did time for arson, Tennessee being one of the few states that charges for arson if it was started as a result of your reckless actions."

Laura wiped the tears from her eyes again. She leaned forward, propping her elbows on her knees and holding her head in her hands. Her shoulders trembled as she sobbed. Pupcake stood and squeezed into Eliza's lap instead.

"Well, that makes sense. He did say that they would disown him completely if they knew about the secret," Laura said. She recounted the one phone conversation she had with her assumed boyfriend after he was arrested.

"I guess his parents never knew it was him, but Sharon knew. She had this massive guilt about keeping this secret all these years, and she planned to head straight to Smallville after the interview," Laura continued, her voice thick with emotion.

"The truly crazy part is that Carter- Peter- I'm never going to get that right... actually tried to capitalize on this whole thing. As if murdering his sister wasn't enough, he was posting this whole amateur documentary idea on YouTube. That's why he wanted to come here so badly to meet you guys." She stopped and cried quietly for a few minutes.

"And that's why he sent the collar for Pupcake that had a camera in it. He wanted the actual death on video," Dean said. "That's crazy."

"Yep," Laura chimed in. "The ridiculous part is that the police were able to hack into the video and he is front and center for the first two seconds setting the thing up. Literally, his face is the first thing you see in the little video clip."

"Are you kidding?!" Dalton exclaimed. "What an idiot!"

"The whole thing is just crazy," Dean said. "He put so much thought and planning into this."

"I know!" Eliza agreed. "The cranberry sugar was kind of brilliant, looking back. He sent a variety of flavored sugars, but only one packet of what he knew would be her favorite. He knew she loved cranberry sugar, so he made sure to put it in front of her." Eliza shook her head.

"And what about meeting Laura? He had to track her down and get her to fall for him just so he could come back and film the scene of the crime." Dean said.

"What a creep," Dalton replied.

Laura continued crying. Dalton pulled her head onto his shoulder, patting her upper back.

"It turns out," Laura said, her voice somewhat muffled from Dalton's shirt against her lips. "He wasn't even registered at the university." She paused, wiping her tears with a tissue without lifting her head from Dalton's shoulder. "I am so gullible," she said. "It's so embarrassing."

"No, honey," Eliza said. "You should not be embarrassed. This guy was psychotic. Let him go, and don't blame yourself. Please, if anything I feel guilty seeing you dragged into this, especially when he played with your emotions like he did."

"That's right, Laura," Dean said. "Promise me you're not going to talk to him anymore, even if he calls."

Laura nodded. "I promise," she said meekly. Then, lifting her head and looking at her brother, then her dad, then her mom, she said, "Thank you guys for being so amazing. I love all of you so much."

"We love you too, honey," Eliza said and the guys agreed. "We'll get through this together. You're not alone."

"Group hug," Dean said, bending down in front of the three of them, arms outstretched. The family leaned in to hug each other, laughing as Pupcake squeezed into the middle, his neck stretched long to get as close as he could.

Eliza's life was coming back together again, and her heart was filled with gratitude. The false rumors that swirled around Copeland were traded out for facts as the news spread, and The Pupcake Café had a line out the door the first day the shop was reopened.

Pupcake himself was happy once again. He was back to spending his days guarding the shop and serving the customers at The Pupcake Café with a friendly wag of the tail.

The café's customers were so generous with their compliments and their tips. Eliza's lemon tart cupcakes were a huge hit, only second to the café's famous strawberry cream cheese cupcakes - the ones that won the blue ribbon.

And speaking of the blue ribbon, Steve from the *Sugar and Spice* magazine reached out to Eliza earlier that day, right after the news of Peter's arrest became public knowledge and offered to return to the café to finish the interview they started.

Although flattered, Eliza politely declined. She just wanted her quiet life back. She didn't want any more fame, and she had all the fortune she could ever need.

———ell———

For an alternate ending filled with unexpected twists and deeper secrets, visit marybbarbee.com/pupcake-alternate -endings/to uncover how Eliza's story could have taken a different turn.

———ell———

Have you read the prequel to *The Pupcake Mystery Series* yet? The beginning of Eliza and Pupcake's journey as amateur sleuths truly begins with *Cupcakes and Corruption*. This story is about a baking competition that turns sour with suspicion of sweet sabotage. And like, *Sweet Suspicion*, there's a shocking twist at the end followed by an alternate ending. You can grab your copy at marybbarb ee.com.

About the Author

Mary B. Barbee is the creative mind behind *The Pupcake Mystery Series*, accompanied by her own loyal chihuahua sidekick, Valentino, who adds a touch of canine flair to every investigation.

With a penchant for crafting stories that keep readers guessing until the very last page, Mary B. enjoys filling her books with quirky characters, small-town settings and, of course, plenty of twists and turns that will keep you on the edge of your seat.

When not writing, Mary B. is either playing a couple sets of tennis or a strategy board game with her two witty daughters and her kindly competitive mother. The four of them share a home in the Inland Northwest in the beautiful town of Spokane, Washington with their really cute - but sometimes naughty - chihuahua.

Mary loves to hear from her readers. Connect at:

marybbarbee@gmail.com
www.facebook.com/marybbarbee
Instagram @marybbarbee
www.marybbarbee.com

More Books to Read By Mary B. Barbee

THE AMISH LANTERN MYSTERY SERIES

Thick As Thieves – Book 1

Robberies are running rampant in Little Valley, and the quiet small-town lives of the Amish community are suddenly thrown into chaos.

Secrets in Little Valley – Book 2

With the bishop's daughter suddenly missing and a new sheriff in town, Anna and Beth find themselves roped into solving another mystery in their small town.

Saving Grace – Book 3

The Amish community in Little Valley is facing big changes, and big threats, with tourism booming. It becomes clear that some of the new businesses want control of the market, and it looks like they are willing to go to great lengths to get it.

Good Intentions – Book 4

Hazel Thompson is found dead in Little Valley's now-famous Amish Inn, and there's a long list of suspects with plenty of motive.

A Blessing in Disguise – Book 5

Jessica McLean opens shop to find a man has been left for dead on the floor of her diner. Could the crime could be related to Jessica's new relationship with their beloved Matthew Beiler?

Christmas Chaos in Little Valley - Book 6

Beth finds out that the Little Valley library is shutting its doors due to a lack of funding and very disturbing anonymous threats.

<u>THE ABIGAIL BAKER MYSTERY SERIES</u>
Blind Faith – Prequel

Abigail's excitement for her new home is replaced by doom and gloom when she finds out that an unexplained murder has rocked the residents of her new town. And not unusual to her, it's the Amish community that is suspect number one.

Grab your free e-copy of Blind Faith at:
marybbarbee.com/blindfaith

Where Fear Ends – Book 1

A town councilman is found dead by the side of the road in the Amish community of Abigail Baker's new hometown.

A Multitude of Sins – Book 2

When secret notes containing serious threats are unveiled, Abigail wonders if the latest victim could have been hiding a multitude of sins.

A Wing and a Prayer – Book 3 ~ COMING SOON!

<u>THE PUPCAKE MYSTERY SERIES</u>
Cupcakes and Corruption – Prequel

Battling empty-nest syndrome, Eliza finds solace in the company of her adorable chihuahua, Pupcake, and her dreams of opening a quaint coffee shop. Little does she know that her talent for baking and nurturing also extends to amateur sleuthing.

Grab your free e-copy of Cupcakes and Corruption at:
marybbarbee.com/pupcakeprequel

Sweet Suspicion – Book 1

The charming town of Copeland is buzzing with excitement as Eliza and her adorable chihuahua, Pupcake, open their new coffee shop. But when a body is discovered on the premises, the duo must put down their baking tools and pick up their detective hats.

Confections and Clues – Book 2

Recipe for Reckoning – Book 3 ~ COMING SOON!

Find excerpts, purchase links and more at
www.marybbarbee.com